GIBRALTAR PASSAGE

Books by T. Davis Bunn

The Maestro
The Presence
Promises to Keep
The Quilt
Riders of the Pale Horse

The Priceless Collection

1. *Florian's Gate*
2. *The Amber Room*
3. *Winter Palace*

Rendezvous With Destiny

1. *Rhineland Inheritance*
2. *Gibraltar Passage*

T. DAVIS BUNN

GIBRALTAR PASSAGE

BETHANY HOUSE PUBLISHERS
MINNEAPOLIS, MINNESOTA 55438

This story is entirely a creation of the author's imagination. No
parallel between any persons, living or dead, is intended.

Cover by Joe Nordstrom

Published by Bethany House Publishers
A Ministry of Bethany Fellowship, Inc.
11300 Hampshire Avenue South
Minneapolis, Minnesota 55438

Printed in the United States of America

Library of Congress Cataloging-in-Publication Data

Bunn, T. Davis, 1952–
    Gibraltar passage / T. Davis Bunn.
        p. cm.   — (Rendezvous with destiny ; bk. 2)
    1. Germany—History—1945–1955—Fiction.
2. Man-woman relationships—Fiction.
3. Europe—History—1945– —Fiction.
4. French—Germany—Fiction. 5. Brothers—Fiction. I. Title.
II. Series: Bunn, T. Davis, 1952– Rendezvous with destiny ; 2.
PS3552.U4718G53   1994   94–6903
813'.54—dc20   CIP
ISBN 1–55661–380–6

This book is dedicated to all our friends at Bethany House Publishers and the Bethany Fellowship. One of the great joys of this relationship is the opportunity it grants us to work with friends. Thank you for allowing us to be a part of your fellowship and mission.

T. DAVIS BUNN, originally of North Carolina, spent many years in Europe as an international business executive. Fluent in several languages, his successful career took him to over 40 countries of the world. But in recent years his faith and his love of writing have come together for a new direction in his life, and *Gibraltar Passage* is his tenth published novel. This extraordinarily gifted novelist is able to create characters and events for a high-powered political novel as well as touch readers' hearts with a quiet yet compelling story like *The Quilt*. He and his wife, Isabella, currently make their home in Oxford, England.

Chapter One

M ajor Pierre Servais, commander of the French garrison at Badenburg, wore a face that frowned from forehead to collar. At the sound of Jake's jeep, Pierre turned from his inspection of work on the refugee camp's sentry towers, walked over, and said, "First we worry because the ground is hard as iron. Now the thaw arrives and we find ourselves working in quicksand."

Lieutenant Colonel Jake Burnes, commander of the U.S. military base at Karlsruhe, watched the team of sweating soldiers struggle to steady a crosspiece while working in mud up to midthigh. "Maybe you ought to wait for the ground to dry out."

"I can't. The entire area has become treacherous. My sentries can no longer even stand, much less walk the perimeter. We must have these elevated positions." Pierre inspected his friend. "From your expression, I take it you could not convince her to stay."

"I didn't even see her," Jake replied. "She left Berlin the day before I arrived. General's orders."

"I am very sorry for you." Pierre reached over and patted his friend's shoulder. "She was posted back to America?"

"Six months," Jake said, her letter burning through his jacket pocket to sear his chest. "On the road almost the whole time. I can't even go see her because I don't know where she'll be. The whole business is classified. A great opportunity, she called it." He resisted the urge to pound the steering wheel. Again. "What does she call our relationship? A burden?"

"Sally must trust you very much," Pierre said solemnly.

"Or just not care one way or the other."

"That is not so, and you know it," Pierre countered. "What will you do?"

"I still have close to a month's leave. Almost wish I didn't now."

"Perhaps you would like to go home?"

"That's what the leave is supposed to be for. But there's not much for me to go home to, remember? My folks are both gone, and my brother didn't make it back from Normandy."

"I meant home with me," Pierre replied.

Jake showed a spark of interest. "To France?"

"That is where home was the last time I looked," Pierre said. "I have received another letter from my mother. She says that I have let the memories block my return for too long."

"You mean about your brother?" Pierre's twin had fought with the Resistance and had died in the war's final months.

"Among other things," Pierre said, his frown deepening. "Come. I need to check the other team's progress."

Jake sprang from his jeep and fell into step alongside his friend. He searched his memory and recalled references to a woman named Jasmyn who had betrayed

Pierre during the war by taking up with a Nazi officer. Jake smiled grimly. He and Pierre made quite a pair.

Their way took them along the internment camp's outer fence. The open fields that had formerly bordered the Badenburg main base had been restructured as a holding center for paperless refugees.

Throughout the fierce winter of 1945–46, central Europe had remained awash in a human flood. Most refugees carried little or no identification, beyond perhaps the tattooed identity numbers of the concentration camp victims. Others were stragglers from farther east, uprooted by the invading of Stalinist forces and flung helter-skelter westward. Few families were intact. Husbands sought wives, wives children, children parents. Mornings in the camp were scarred by the wails rising from the Red Cross center when the daily reports confirmed that those being sought were no more.

Such camps were seas of humanity encircled by barbed wire. There was never enough room, or food or medicine, or news from the lands now suffering under Stalin's mighty fist. By midwinter, the number of homeless refugees in the American sector of the former Third Reich had risen to more than two million. The French sector had been similarly inundated.

The spring thaw had reduced the sentries' path to a muddy bog. Jake and Pierre stayed on the grassy verge and picked their way carefully as they skirted the camp. Jake resisted the urge to return the never-ending stares from behind the fence.

As they rounded the corner, a cry from somewhere inside the camp made Jake wince. No matter how often he heard the sound, he could not become hardened to the tragedy of another refugee's loss of hope. He steeled himself and continued onward until he realized that Pierre was no longer at his side.

Jake turned around to find his friend staring at the fence with a gaze of hollow agony.

Again there was the cry, and this time Jake heard it as a name. "Patrique!" Pierre recoiled as though taking a blow to the heart.

Jake spotted a girl struggling through the dense lines of bearded men and kerchiefed women waiting for food. The people were reluctant to let her through, both because of their obvious hunger and because a step in the wrong direction meant moving off the boardwalk and stepping into the mud. She ignored their complaints and curses, shoving and wriggling and fighting toward the fence. "Patrique!"

Pierre moved toward the fence, did not notice where he stepped, and sank to his knees in the bog.

The girl extricated herself from the final line, and promptly slipped and fell headlong into the mire. She scarcely seemed to notice. Even before the fall was complete, she was battling to right herself. Her feet spun for a hold in the slick mud. The front of her dress was encrusted. Dirt streaked her dark hair and painted one emaciated cheek. Finally she recovered her footing and flung herself at the fence. She thrust her face and one hand through the wire and screamed in a broken voice, "Patrique!"

A sentry called out a warning and started forward. Pierre barked out a command in French, but did not seem to have the strength to free himself from the bog. Jake walked over and offered a hand. "What's going on?"

Pierre accepted the help without really seeing. He

mumbled something in French, his eyes fastened on the screaming girl.

"Try that in English, buddy," Jake told him.

Pierre swung around, seemed to have trouble remembering who Jake was. Then he said in a benumbed voice, "Patrique was my brother."

Chapter Two

J ake sat in the corner of what once had been Colonel
Beecham's office but now belonged to Pierre Servais.
The former American base at Badenburg was presently
a central French garrison, with Pierre as acting commandant. Pierre sat behind his desk, his hands shaking
so hard he could scarcely bring the cup to his lips. Jake
watched him listen to the girl's story, hoping that Pierre
would begin to recover from the shock of having heard
the young girl call out his dead brother's name. But if
anything, Pierre was becoming continually more dis-
traught. The young French major winced at the girl's
voice. His own questions were hoarse and hesitant.

The girl was barely able to speak around her tears.
It was hard to tell her age because she suffered from the
refugees' most common ailment—desperate hunger.
The skin of her face was like dry parchment, stretched
tightly over bones of birdlike fragility. Her brown eyes
watched a strange and dangerous world from dark-
lined cavities. Yet her whole being burned with an in-
tensity that belied her frailty. Jake imagined that given
a chance to recover, she would emerge as a raven-haired
beauty.

Seventeen, Jake decided, listening to her continue the

halting discourse with Pierre. Maybe a year older. She spoke German with the lilting tone he had come to recognize as the result of speaking Yiddish at home. Neither her sadness nor the urgency of her words could obscure her voice's musical quality.

Her name was Lilliana Goss, she told them. She was half Jewish, half German. It was her mother who taught her Yiddish. Although she had been raised in a Christian home, her mother had insisted on keeping her Jewish heritage alive. Her father, a former university professor, had managed to bribe their way out of Germany when the Nazi sweeps intensified.

"My father was in contact with the Resistance across the border in France," she told Pierre. "That is what saved us. We were taken to Marseille, and from there to Morocco. We met Patrique, your brother, in Marrakesh. My father began working with him, processing the incoming refugees, arranging for false papers, keeping on the lookout for spies and turncoats.

"My father's health started to fail. I began helping out more and more with Patrique's operations. I became a local messenger for the group and helped to forge documents. I had nothing else to do with my time, and I enjoyed the feeling of being useful. One night, a few months before Morocco was liberated—"

"When exactly," Pierre grated.

She thought a moment. "The first week in April," she replied with confidence. "I remember because my birthday had been only a few days before."

The news visibly shook Pierre. "Go on."

"I was working alone in our offices, they were hidden under the eaves of the Red Cross building, when Patrique rushed in. He startled me, because he had been called away in March. Nobody knew where he was.

There had been all sorts of rumors floating around about how he had been captured or killed, but I had refused to believe them."

Pierre was taking the story very hard. The longer Lilliana continued, the more he seemed to shrink inside himself. Jake watched him, recalled the day news had come of his own brother's death on the Normandy beaches, and ached for his friend.

"Patrique was furious to find me there. I did not understand his anger, because I had feared the worst and was overjoyed to see him alive. He said that a messenger was to have met him that night but had not arrived at the meeting point. Patrique had waited three hours, then risked going to the offices, where he found me. Since I knew nothing about a messenger, Patrique was forced to assume that the French conspirators had captured him."

Pierre roused himself enough to rasp out, "You mean the Nazis."

Lilliana responded with an adamant shake of her dark locks. "He said the French. I asked the same thing. He *insisted* it was the French, which made him extremely distressed. But he refused to explain. He said the less I knew the better. Then he asked me if I would take on a dangerous assignment. He hated to use me, but there was no one else, and he had to leave that very night. He knew the forces were hard on his trail. I adored your brother and would have done anything for him. He asked me to take a message to his friends in Marseille. He said a boat was waiting for his messenger in the Tangiers harbor. I was to go there, take the boat, deliver the message, and return immediately."

Again Pierre stirred himself enough to ask, "What was the message?"

"Beware the traitor," the girl replied, "I have the proof you need."

"Which traitor?" Pierre demanded.

"Patrique did not say," Lilliana replied. "Only that it was no longer safe for him in Morocco. That he was going to try to make it to Gibraltar. And that they should not believe overmuch in rumors of his death."

Two days after finding Lilliana, Jake and Pierre boarded the train for Marseille. Lilliana had been examined by the local Red Cross doctors and proclaimed unfit for travel—acute malnourishment and a persistent low-grade fever. Besides which there was still no word from her family. Three inquiries had been sent to Morocco, with no reply. Pierre's last action before departing had been to place yet another request through official channels.

The train was crammed to overflowing. Every compartment was full. People jammed the aisles outside, sitting on their luggage, standing, crushed together like sardines. Yet there was no pushing, no shoving, no arguments over places. With their officers' passes, Pierre and Jake were assured seats. Twice they rose and tried to give their places to ladies. Both times they were refused—not only by the women themselves but by all the people surrounding them. When the people saw that Jake did not understand their words, they motioned him down with hand signals. Sit, sit. Officers deserved a place.

Of Pierre they asked as much as politeness allowed. Where were the gentlemen coming from? And where, might one ask, were they headed? Ah, Marseille. A beautiful city. To see the family. How nice. And the first time since the end of the war? Oh, how exciting it must be for you, sir. And for your friend, this will be his first time in France? Welcome, welcome. Smiles and bows were presented in Jake's direction. May your stay in France be a glorious one. That was the word they used, Pierre assured him. A *glorious* stay. This from people who wore their hunger as evidently as the frayed elbows and carefully darned tears in their clothes. They wished him a glorious stay in their beloved land.

Once they were settled in their seats, Jake asked Pierre in a low voice, "Why did you keep asking Lilliana to repeat parts of her story, you know, about when Patrique came back to Morocco unexpectedly?"

"Because, my friend," Pierre replied, "this entire episode took place a month after my brother was supposed to have died."

Jake turned back toward the train window and mulled this over. The others in their compartment showed polite disinterest, granting them as much privacy as their crowded surroundings would allow.

Lilliana's story had not ended there. She had done as Patrique had requested, traveled to Marseille, and hurried to the designated address. But the building had been destroyed in the war, and she had no other way of contacting Pierre's friends. In desperation she had walked the streets until a roving German patrol spotted her and arrested her for being out after curfew. She soon found herself on a train with other detainees, heading north.

Once inside Germany, the train had been halted and left to languish on a siding for three days. Finally the soldiers in charge had forced those still alive to continue onward by foot. They had walked for a very long time—

Lilliana was not sure exactly how long, the days had melted together. She had ended up in a workers' camp and endured the grueling weeks of autumn and winter working in an unheated bomb factory. Then with the spring had come the Allied liberators, and after that she had been passed from one camp to another, awaiting papers and word of her family.

"I am tempted to travel directly to Gibraltar," Pierre broke in, "but I know I must first go to my family in Marseille."

"I thought you said they were in—" Jake searched his memory, but could not recall the name. "Some other town."

"Montpelier," Pierre supplied. "My family originally came from Marseille, and we spent much time there when I was growing up. During the war my parents moved back there because survival was easier when surrounded by family. Now my uncle, my mother's brother, is one of the President's team in Marseille. Not one of the cabinet, mind you. One of the local staff. He is in charge of food distribution for that area of Provence. My father works with him. Marseille is where the Americans offload all supplies."

As soon as he had recovered from Lilliana's story, Pierre had applied for and been granted long-overdue leave to visit his family. The brigadier general responsible for Jake's region had then personally authorized his own travel to France—not because of Pierre, but because he knew of Jake's lack of family and his distress over Sally.

The train that took them through the Alsace countryside was from a bygone era. Plumes of smoke and cinders flew by their closed window. Jake gave thanks for a chilly day. If it had been warmer and the windows open, they would both have arrived blackened by the chuffing locomotive.

"Gibraltar," Pierre murmured. "Why would he choose to go there, of all places? Why not home?"

"It seems to me that if your brother really had survived," Jake cautioned, "he would have gotten in touch with somebody long before now."

"Do not rob me of hope, my friend," Pierre said, his eyes still on the countryside. "Already it hangs from the slenderest of threads. Do not swing the knife."

"I just—"

"Don't," Pierre repeated, turning away from the window. "Let me sit for now, this moment, this day, and believe that there might indeed be a chance that Patrique is still alive. My mind too is full of all the arguments, but my heart does not wish to hear them. Not now. Not yet."

Jake nodded his understanding. "So tell me more about your brother."

Pierre was silent a long moment, then began. "Marseille is a funny place. For the first three years of the war, it was occupied by the Italians. Between the mentality of the Italians and that of the Marseille people, life there was what we call 'soft.' People got on with the business of living. There was laughter. There was smuggling. That is what my brother did. He smuggled bodies."

"Warm ones, I hope."

Pierre smiled. "My brother operated the Marseille end of an underground system that smuggled out people wanted by the Nazis. About half were Jews. The others were mostly German intelligentsia, people who publicly opposed Hitler's madness—professionals, priests, teachers, writers. He was very successful, my brother. At least, as long as the Italians were there."

"After that?"

"After that, well, after that came the Nazis. And life became very hard."

"And your brother?"

"Patrique stayed for as long as he could. Then one night the Nazis came for him, and we all thought he had been taken. But somehow he had managed to escape at the very last moment. He went to Morocco and operated there for a while."

Jake inspected his friend's somber face. "He was killed there?"

"So we were told," Pierre sighed. "Where exactly I have not been able to determine. Everything after his departure from Marseille remains a mystery."

Jake said quietly, "You miss him."

"There is a bond between twins that only another twin can understand," Pierre said. "It is for me like an invisible connection from the womb. More than sympathy. We *share* in the emotions and the experiences of one another. Across distances, across time. We are different, yet the same."

Jake listened and heard the way his friend spoke. We *are* these things, Pierre was saying. Not were. Not in the past. Still today. Jake heard, and understood, and dared hope for his friend as he had not been able to hope for his own family.

"I am the cautious one. Reserved. Deliberate. I am the one who made the good army officer," Pierre continued. "Patrique is bold. More than that. He is reckless. I was the reins that held Patrique in place. I think he understood this better than I. Through Patrique I felt the emotions I never allowed myself, and through me

Patrique knew a balance between caution and abandon."

The emotions that etched themselves on Pierre's features were too naked for Jake to feel comfortable watching. He turned his attention to the window, listening carefully, but granting his friend the only privacy he could offer.

"Patrique was younger than me," Pierre continued, pitching his voice softly. With the noise of the locomotive and the train's rattles and squeaks, only Jake could hear him. "He was younger only by two minutes in time, but always I was the older brother. I went through life feeling that I watched over him. I was responsible for him. I was the rock. Patrique was the wind."

The train did not go fast. Nothing seemed to move fast in this land. The entire country appeared to be gradually recovering from shock, stumbling a bit as it found its footing.

Their journey was one of stark contrasts. Some towns and villages were left virtually untouched by the war, at least as far as Jake could see. Others were pitifully scarred. All wore the same run-down look as the people.

"When Patrique was fifteen," Pierre told Jake, "he got a job working at the local hippodrome, the racetrack. He became an excellent rider. In his free time, he began hunting the wild white stallions of the Camargue. I can still remember him flying across the great salt flats, both hands busy with his lasso, guiding his horse with his knees. The weekends he went hunting, my mother used to spend at the local *église*, praying that her son would come home in one piece.

"Patrique sought out the Resistance within days of the German invasion," Pierre went on. "He proposed that they use the hippodrome as a gathering point for the fleeing refugees. In his first letter to me, he bragged that already they had ten times as many Jews as horses in the stables. It gave him great pride to help these people."

Pierre was silent for a time, then said to himself, "I think I have always seen my brother as the hero I never was."

"That's crazy and you know it," Jake protested. "Where did you get those medals on your chest, a bazaar?"

The journey from Karlsruhe to Strasbourg to Lyons to Marseille took twenty-eight hours. For the majority of the trip, Pierre remained immersed in his thoughts and his memories. Jake did not complain. His own ruminations were more than enough company. At times he would emerge, look about, return the smiles of the people whose eye he caught. But soon enough the blanket of sorrowful thoughts tucked itself up tight around his chest and he retreated into missing Sally.

Six months. The time stretched out before him in endless emptiness. It did not matter how much he argued with himself. It did not matter that she had been ordered to go. It did not matter that her work was important. Jake found it impossible to see beyond the painful fact that she was not there beside him.

Near Avignon the train chuffed around a high rock ledge just as the sun cleared the horizon. Gray-faced rocks drank in the morning light and were transformed into shades of soft coral. The train's brakes squealed on a sharp decline, the whistle blew a greeting to the new day, and they were swallowed by the ancient town.

From Avignon the train followed the Rhone River's winding path, never leaving its side for more than a few minutes. The air was scented with olive trees and pines and awakening spring. The sensation of entering a new world grew ever stronger. Behind them northern Europe still struggled to cast off winter's cloak. Here in the Provence, spring had long since been welcomed home with open arms.

The faces surrounding Jake seemed to lose some of their deeper lines. Eyes shadowed by years of strain and worry and war took on a glint of newfound humor as breakfast provisions were brought out. The woman next to Jake unfolded a checkered bundle to reveal a round loaf of bread, home-whipped butter, and a honeycomb in waxed paper. Shyly she offered him a portion. The entire compartment watched as he bit and chewed, then shared a smile as he moaned his pleasure.

Jake offered his handful to Pierre. "You want some?"

"What?" Startled by the words, he turned from his endless perusal of the window. "Oh, no thank you."

"It's great."

The woman next to Jake spoke up, urging Pierre to take a portion. He dredged up a smile and shook his head. Pierre remained the only one of their compartment untouched by the new day.

He felt Jake's eyes on him and turned a sorrowful gaze toward his friend. "I was thinking of Jasmyn."

Once more Jake recalled late-night talks. "She's the woman who betrayed you by taking up with a Nazi officer, right?"

His friend nodded and confessed, "The closer we come to Marseille, the harder it is to keep the memory of her behind me. You remember how I said that there could never be another woman for me?"

"I remember," Jake said quietly.

Pierre sighed his way back to the window. "All she did, all that was, and still I yearn for her."

"Would it help to talk?"

"Thank you, my friend," Pierre replied to the unseen day outside the train. "But more words about Jasmyn would be lances to my spirit."

Outside Arles, a new conductor made his way down the crowded train. He was an ancient survivor of the First War, the chest of his heavy blue conductor's uniform sporting three rows of ribbons. When they handed over their official passes, the old man drew himself to attention and threw them a rusty salute.

For the first time that morning, Pierre showed a spark of life. He asked the old man a question and received an overloud reply. Pierre smiled, only his eyes holding the stain of unspoken memories. He motioned toward Jake and spoke at length. All eyes in the compartment turned his way. Pierre pointed to the ribbons on Jake's own chest and gave a name to several of them. His words were greeted with appreciative oohs and aahs.

Jake objected with, "You mind telling me—"

But Pierre cut him off with further words in French. He grew fervent, his voice rising to reach more of the passengers who now crowded into the compartment's open door. The woman seated next to him had eyes as wide as saucers. Jake felt his face grow hot.

The ancient conductor handed back Jake's papers and snapped off a second salute. Jake accepted the papers and brushed one hand across the front of his close-cropped hair. The conductor spun around, shut the compartment door behind him, and talked excitedly with the people jamming the corridor who immediately crowded around him. From the looks cast through the smudged glass partition, Jake assumed the old man was recounting Pierre's story.

Jake leaned forward and muttered, "What was that all about?"

"I was simply telling them a little of who you are," Pierre replied.

Jake shot a glance toward the growing number of faces pressed against the glass. "You don't say."

"Believe me, I was defusing trouble before it could take hold," Pierre replied. "Not everyone you meet in Marseille greets Americans as friends."

"Why is that?"

"There was a terrible bombing here in 1944," Pierre answered. "The city's worst destruction from the entire war."

"By the Americans?"

Pierre nodded. "The Allies decided the city was important enough to be bombed, since Marseille was a German submarine harbor. They wanted to destroy three points—the central train station, a storage center, and the submarine base. The Americans came with their great bombers called Superfortresses. But not one bomb found its target. Not one. Bombs fell all over the city. The worst destruction was in the Quartier Saint Charles, not far from the station. Over three thousand people were killed that night, all within two hours. It was tragic. The city's highest death toll in all the years of war."

Jake sat back in his seat. "I'm really sorry, Pierre."

His friend replied with another smile that did not reach his eyes. "In some ways, the city of Marseille is but a very large village. By tomorrow it will be known all through the markets that a great American hero has come to visit their beloved town. And that he will stay in the home of their own Resistance hero, the famous Patrique Servais."

Marseille was a bustling, thriving city. It was also a city wed firmly to the sea. The Bay of Marseille bit out a mighty chunk, as vast as a great inland lake. Hills rose on the north and east, giving the impression from seaside that the entire town looked out upon water. The deep blue Mediterranean waters caught the sun's rays and brushed the tired land with hope of a new tomorrow.

As the train wound its way toward the station, Pierre pointed out a great medieval castle, rising from the city's southern tip. It was the Fortress of Saint John, he said, from which Crusade ships journeyed into the unknown dangers of the Ottoman Empire.

The train platform was jammed solid. When Pierre stepped into view, a great cry of joy arose from the throng. He was immediately swept into a huge crowd of laughing, crying, singing, shouting people. Jake stood on the train's top step and watched as a diminutive woman in black stepped forward. The crowd quieted and drew back a step as she reached up one age-scarred hand to stroke the side of Pierre's face. When Pierre reached down and enveloped the woman, a second great cheer arose. He reached out behind the woman and made room in the embrace for a bespectacled man who held his sparse frame rigidly erect. Tears streamed from every face in view.

A champagne cork popped, then another, and suddenly every hand was holding a mug, a cup, a glass. Pierre turned to find Jake still standing at the crowd's periphery and shouted for silence. He waved Jake over and said in English, "Come join me, my friend."

A space was made through which Jake walked. Pierre raised his voice and spoke briefly in French, ending with the words, "Colonel Jake Burnes." A murmur of greeting rose in reply.

"These are friends and family," Pierre explained. "Many have traveled from Montpelier to welcome me home."

Pierre's mother reached over and gripped Jake's arm with surprising strength. She spoke rapidly, her voice trembling slightly, her eyes shining despite the tears.

"My mother tells me to apologize for her lack of English," Pierre translated. For this moment at least, the shadows were gone from his eyes. "I am to tell you that she has read from my letters about your parents' accident and the loss of your brother in the war, and that she grieves for you. She says that she would consider it an honor if you would consider our family to be your own."

A pewter mug full of champagne was thrust into Jake's hand. A great salute rose as Pierre raised his own cup and toasted the crowd and his parents. Then he turned to Jake and said, "Welcome home, my friend."

Chapter Three

J ake awoke to the sound of church bells clanging directly beside his head.

He groped his way upright, rubbed his eyes, and realized that the bells were ringing through his open window. He stumbled across the room, but just as his hand gripped the ledge the clanging stopped. The air ached with the sudden stillness.

Thoroughly awake, Jake took in his surroundings. The Servais family did not live in the city of Marseille itself, but in Le Rouet, a small farming village near both the city and the sea. The village church stood to Jake's right, bordering the cobblestone plaza. To his left rose houses so old they appeared to have grown naturally from the earth. Beyond the village stretched vast fields of verdant green.

Jake leaned on the windowsill and watched the gentle colors strengthen into full-fledged day. Great wild birch and umbrella pines acted as natural windbreaks for the ancient houses. Hoopoes and robins and nightingales and song thrushes sang the glory of Pierre's homecoming.

Through his window Jake saw a fox shepherd her three cubs across the field. Herons stood in white calmness about the edge of a distant lake. Flamingos fed with the foolish intricacy of ballet dancers. Ducks mocked all Jake's worries. Beyond the fields and lake stretched the wetlands, silver-white with salt.

His attention was drawn downward at the sound of a closing door. He watched as Pierre's father and mother, dressed in suit and dress of basic black, exited the house and walked arm in arm toward the chapel.

Pierre swung the bedroom door open. "Ah, you're awake. Good."

"It'd be easier to sleep through D-day than that racket."

"Yes, my father says he has never found it so easy to be on time for morning Mass." Although the joy of yesterday's homecoming had dimmed, Pierre's sardonic smile appeared to be firmly in place. "I spent much of last night going over places we need to check. Shall we get started?"

"Give me two minutes to throw on some clothes," Jake replied, "and I'm with you."

First stop was the port of Marseille. The harbor seemed to be flourishing. Fishing vessels of every size and make bustled in smoky confusion between the great gray hulks of the American battleships. With the Sixth Fleet using Marseille as a major center for offloading supplies, the streets were full of American uniforms.

Tankers and cargo vessels lay at anchor or vied for space at the crowded docks. The surrounding streets were jammed with every imaginable form of transport, from donkey carts to military trucks to human-powered pushcarts. People shouted and cursed and fought their way through the crawling traffic. The air stank from rotting fish and seaweed, from the refuse of a thousand broken food crates, from the fumes of the overheated trucks.

Pierre did a slow circle, took a deep breath, and smiled with vast pleasure. "Ah, my friend, it is so good to be home!"

Alleys opening off the main thoroughfares widened into markets selling everything from fish to fashionable clothes, from seaweed fertilizer to silverware. Time after time Pierre and Jake's progress was stopped by stall holders who dropped their wares, shoved aside impatient customers, and rushed to greet Pierre with cries of welcome. Large women swathed in layers of frayed sweaters and stained with fish scales enveloped Pierre in their fleshy arms, tears of joy streaming down their broad faces. Old fishermen overturned packing crates and scattered ice and nets in their haste to rush over and pound his back.

Each time Pierre extricated himself from their blows, he pointed toward Jake and spoke an introduction. They turned and doffed battered berets, their hands curled into stone-hard rigidity by decades of fighting nets and fish. Leathery seams creased until dark eyes almost disappeared, and smiles revealed a few remaining smoke-stained teeth. Then Jake was pulled into the back-slapping circle, where his total lack of French in no way slowed down the questions thrown his way. Jake replied with shrugs and smiles, while Pierre tried to keep up with a dozen people demanding answers at once.

Whenever the name of Patrique was brought up, the crowd quieted. A moment of reflecting upon the ground, the sky, the harbor's scummy waters, and then quietly Pierre would ask his question. Eyes widened, the group tightened, voices tensed. Jake watched faces, since he could not understand the talk, and repeatedly saw a struggle pass over their weather-beaten features. They drank in Pierre's news with breathless unease. They wanted to believe, tried to believe. But in the end they turned away with sorrowful shakes of their heads. Patrique, to their minds, was no more.

"They don't know anything," Jake said with certainty when they stopped for a breather at a harbor cafe. The air was redolent with the pungent odor of French cigarettes and cheap wine. Jake followed Pierre's example and hunched down over his coffee. That appeared to be the universal signal for privacy, and no one approached them unless one or the other straightened up.

"I think you are right," Pierre said. "No one has heard anything to suggest Patrique is alive."

"You don't seem surprised."

"No," he agreed. "If Patrique had made it this far, the family would have heard. Of this I am sure."

"Then why are you doing this?"

"Planting seeds," Pierre replied. "All I need is for one to grow and bear fruit. The fishermen and the smugglers and these local traders often work together, you see. There is the chance that someone stopped somewhere to pick up an illegal shipment and heard something which he discounted."

"Up to now," Jake added.

"Exactly. So he hears that Pierre is back and is spreading word that Patrique might be alive. Of course, most people will say it is a futile hope, but who knows what might turn up?"

"They all seem to think a lot of you."

"Patrique and I both worked as boys on fishing boats," Pierre said. "We had an uncle who was a fisherman, and he used to tell us stories of foreign ports and mysteries of the sea. My father is a very wise man. He knew that if he was to forbid our going to sea, we would both have run away. So instead he urged us to spend our summers working for my uncle. Although we learned to love the sea, we also learned that the hard life of a fisherman was not for us."

Pierre sipped his coffee, then continued. "When the Resistance was starting here, Patrique used his old connections to organize those smugglers and fishermen who wished to help. When I was home on leave, I worked with him."

"Patrique led the local Resistance?"

"There was no single leader. Cells, or units, were formed. Patrique worked with a number of these units."

Jake decided he could ask what had been on his mind since his arrival. "Will you tell your parents what you've learned?"

"My father only," Pierre replied, his face somber. "I told him last night. He agrees we must say nothing of this to my mother."

"That's probably wise."

"Losing Patrique almost killed her. We cannot speak with her until we know for certain, and then only with the greatest caution." He dug in his pocket, tossed a coin on the counter, and rose to his feet. "Come, let us go plant some more seeds."

They exited the cafe, crossed the main port road, passed through a tiny arched portal, and descended a dozen grime-encrusted stairs into a miniature market square. Another shout greeted their entry. Jake held back and watched Pierre being swept up by another joyful crowd.

A gentle tug on his sleeve caught Jake's attention. He turned, the smile in place, expecting to find some ancient fisherman wanting to pump the hand of Pierre's friend.

Instead, he confronted a slender figure covered from head to toe in a great gray cape. The hood was slid so far forward that the face was totally lost in shadow. A honey-coated woman's voice said in English, "Step back away from where he can see us."

"What?" Jake took a reluctant step as the figure backed between two stalls toward the ancient stone wall. When he hesitated to move farther, the figure raised one fine hand and beckoned impatiently.

"Who—"

His words were cut off as the hood was folded back to reveal one of the most beautiful faces he had ever seen.

Great eyes of darkest jade captured him and held him fast. High cheekbones slanted above a finely carved jawline, the sharp features balanced by full red lips. Rich, dark hair was gathered over one shoulder and held by a silver clasp inscribed in a writing that Jake could not fathom.

The eyes. They held him with a sorrowful calmness that stilled his ability to question.

"You are Pierre's friend," she said, her voice as soft and rich as her gaze.

Jake could only nod.

"I am Jasmyn." Her gaze flickered behind him. Slender hands rose to sweep the hood back forward, and the beautiful face was lost once more to the shadows. "We haven't much time, Pierre turns this way. Tonight or tomorrow he will take you to a restaurant called Le Relais des Pêcheurs. There is a cafe next door. I will await you."

"Jake!" Pierre's voice called from amidst the throng.

The hand reached out and grasped his arm with a power that seemed to scald through his uniform. "Do not tell him I have seen you. But come. Please come."

"Jake! Come on over here!"

"I have heard of your search for Patrique," said the hidden woman. "You *must* come. I have news."

Then she swept around and vanished, her absence a vacuum in the bustling market.

Chapter Four

"It's cold tonight," Jake said as they bicycled back into town that evening. Although there were a few cars around, including one used by Pierre's father, petrol was almost impossible to find. Bicycles remained the most popular and dependable means of transport.

"This is the home of the mistrals, the winter winds," Pierre replied, pedaling alongside him. "They funnel down through the Alpine foothills and strike Marseille with brutal force. On nights like this, we say that winter has returned to remind us of what was and what will be again."

Just as Jasmyn had predicted, Pierre had invited him to eat at a restaurant near the harbor, one run by an old friend. But Jake found it difficult to concentrate on the coming meal and their conversation on the way. He found it even harder to keep quiet about Jasmyn's presence in the city. "From the sound of things, you must like this restaurant a lot."

"Marseille is the most ancient town in France," Pierre replied in his roundabout manner. "The Romans used it as the port for all the upper Mediterranean. From the old harbor, when I was growing up, there was a major thoroughfare that split the town into two sections. The one nearest to the old fortress was called Le Panier, the Basket. It was the oldest part of town. Very, very ancient. And very crowded. A lot of bars, prostitutes, fishermen, tiny market areas, very small shops." Pierre waved and smiled a reply to the greeting of an old gentleman seated beside a roadside cafe. "Le Panier was always full of life. The restaurant we are going to tonight is on its border. Whenever I think of Marseille, I think of that area. It was where my brother operated from."

Jake's breath pushed out wispy clouds as they crested a ridge and the harbor came into view. A great-coat that had once belonged to Pierre's brother flapped around his legs as he pedaled. "Why is that?"

"A person who knew the area could remain hidden in the maze of alleys and stairs and passages for a lifetime. It was possible to go from the central train station to the water, a distance of perhaps two kilometers, and never walk upon any road or path that could be found on a map."

"Incredible."

"Yes, exactly that. The entire history of that area was incredible. It was built during the time of the Crusaders, upon ways that had existed since Charlemagne. The second time I visited during the war, my brother took me down what I thought was a blind alley. But there in the back were carved these small stone steps that would go unnoticed unless you knew what you were looking for. Then up above, on top of the wall, a narrow path intersected three small gardens and joined a bridge which from below looked to be merely two overlapping roofs."

"Sounds like an amazing place."

"It was, yes. And there was such a great mixture of

people in that area. Many small-time gangsters, who ran the gambling and the prostitutes. Many shop owners, whose families had been there, probably working the same tiny shop, for hundreds and hundreds of years. And fishermen, extremely conservative families who kept to themselves. Somehow my brother managed to make friends with all those people, and all of them helped him with his smuggling work."

As they approached the water's edge, the evening crowd thickened to the point that the road became impassible even for bicycles. They dismounted and walked.

"So what happened?"

"When the Germans came in, they demolished the entire area. It was impossible to control, so one day they simply went in and leveled it." Pierre swept his hand out. "One day home to several thousand families, the next rubble."

"What happened to the people?"

"Ah, that is another mystery." Pierre stopped and shook the hands of a young couple, exchanged greetings with three others, then rejoined Jake and continued. "According to what we learned later, the Germans planned to round everyone up, interrogate them to find out who was involved in illegal activities—which of course meant almost everyone—then ship them off to the camps. But instead, almost no one was there! The entire area had been cleared out overnight, right under the noses of the Nazi guards. Poof!"

"An informer," Jake guessed.

"Yes, that is what I think as well. But who would have had access to such information? And who could have gotten that information back to so many families so fast?"

Pierre smiled fondly at the ancient facades lining the harbor. "So many mysteries," he murmured. "That is the nature of Marseille, my friend. It is close enough to the Arab world to have learned to treasure its secrets."

Their entry into the restaurant was greeted with a roar of approval. Chairs were shoved aside and napkins flung onto tables as waiters and patrons together rushed forward to hail Pierre Servais. Jake allowed himself to be swept up in the hubbub. His coat was slid from his shoulders, a chair was jammed up behind him, and friendly hands forced him down. A glass was slapped into his hand. A bottle appeared. But just as the room quieted for a toast, a rotund little man in a chef's apron and hat pushed his way through the crowd to stand before their table. His cheeks were the color of ripe apples, and below his nub of a nose sprouted a curling waxed moustache. He sprang to attention, which shoved his belly out at a ridiculous angle, and snapped off a parade-ground salute. "A votre service, mon Capitaine!"

"Major," corrected a voice from the crowd.

"Jake, allow me to present Sergeant Roncard," Pierre told him. "Formerly the greatest scrounger in the Fighting Free French."

"True, true," the rotund little man agreed merrily in English.

"In the middle of the Algerian desert," Pierre went on, "the illustrious sergeant fed his troop so well we actually gained weight."

"I took my duties most seriously, mon Capitaine," Roncard replied, still at attention.

"When my men began wondering if we would ever be permitted to fight, and I was growing weary of fighting for the attention of deaf officers, the grand sergeant told me to invite the general for a dinner. After finishing off the only wine within a hundred kilometers—"

"Two hundred," the little man murmured.

"—not to mention dining on desert grouse and wild onions—"

"Ah, you remember," Roncard said, and stuck out his pigeon's chest even farther.

"—the general was made to see reason, and we were sent into action with the Americans. Not, I must add, without a struggle, for the general wanted to keep the sergeant for himself. The sergeant, being made of hero material, insisted on his right as a French soldier to fight alongside his brothers." Pierre grinned. "After that, our brigade saw more of the general than any other. Not to mention being the first to receive scarce supplies."

"You do me great honor, mon Capitaine."

"None but what you deserve." Pierre rose to his feet and raised his glass. "A toast."

"To a free France," Roncard shouted.

"Vive la France!" cried the room with one great voice.

Jake raised his glass with the others and silently blessed the fate that had brought him here.

A steaming bowl of bouillabaisse was followed by partridge stuffed with mushrooms and cooked in fresh spices, cream, and white wine. Every few minutes Roncard popped back through the kitchen doors to make sure that everything was satisfactory and to apologize for the paltry meal. *Dégoulas,* he moaned, dragging the word out like a chant. How was he to run a first-class restaurant when everything had to be purchased either with coupons or on the black market? When Jake assured the little chef that the meal was the best he had eaten in ages, Roncard puffed up like a pink balloon.

When they had finished, chairs from other tables were drawn closer, and the air soon thickened with the scents of Gauloisie cigarettes and syrupy coffee. Pierre switched to French and began telling his story once more.

Jake stood. "Think maybe I'll get a breath of air."

"Don't stray where there are no lights," Pierre warned. "Marseille is still Marseille."

Then Roncard was at his elbow, leading him toward the door. When they were away from the group of locals, he said quietly, "You are a good friend, Colonel Burnes."

"I try to be."

"Go," he said softly. "She awaits."

That stopped him. "You know about Jasmyn?"

"All know," Roncard said simply. "All know, all approve, all hope against hope."

"I don't understand," Jake replied. "All know about what?"

The little man opened the door and permitted in a breath of fresh night air. "A good friend," he repeated and ushered Jake into the darkness.

The cafe was as crowded as the restaurant, but the atmosphere was more subdued. Jake pushed open the glass portal and squinted to see through the smoke. There in the center was a table made noticeable by its isolation. A woman sat alone, her back to the door, her long dark hair gathered and brought over one slender shoulder. Hers was the only table occupied by one person. The card playing and smoky companionship swirled around her, yet left her untouched.

Jasmyn looked up at Jake's approach. When he stopped before her table, she said quietly, "Thank you for coming, Colonel Burnes."

"I don't even know what I'm doing here."

"Sit down. Please." Her voice was as softly sad as her gaze. As Jake slid into a seat, the barkeeper came around the counter and stopped before their table. His eyes flickered over Jake, then turned to Jasmyn. She asked, "What will you have?"

"Coffee, I guess."

"Café, s'il vous plaît," she said. The bartender gave her a respectful bow and returned to behind the counter.

Jake felt eyes turning his way. He glanced around, saw people at every nearby table watching him speculatively. "What is this all about?"

Jasmyn seemed uncertain as to how to proceed. She fiddled with her spoon, asked, "They say you are a hero."

"I was in the war. I survived. That's true for a lot of people."

"They say your brother died on the beaches at Normandy."

The sudden piercing ache hardened his voice. "It's not my brother we're here to talk about."

A warning appeared in the eyes of those patrons close enough to have heard the change in his voice. Jake held their gaze and had a sudden realization that it was not mere curiosity he saw, nor hostility toward a stranger.

"It means a great deal to these people that you have suffered a loss here in our land."

Jake nodded. He was beginning to understand. They were not isolating them because she was not welcome. They were doing it out of respect. He looked around the tables and saw how faces throughout the room turned their way, then looked away. Checking on her. Watching him carefully. They were *protecting* her. They were protecting *her*.

He asked, "The folks here are friends of yours?"

"I was born and raised in the area of Marseille called Le Panier. You have heard of it?"

"The Basket, sure, Pierre told me how the Germans tore it down."

"Walk one block and you can see the destruction for yourself. Many of these people you see here were scattered to the wind. Now that the war is over, they shall come back and rebuild. This cafe and the restaurant next door are gathering places."

Her face was a remarkable mixture of fragility and strength. Every feature was drawn as with a chisel, clear and distinct. Yet there was a delicacy to her, as though the sorrow in her voice and her eyes could overwhelm her at any moment.

"My father was a fisherman. His family had lived in Le Panier since the Middle Ages. My mother was Moroccan. From a desert tribe. She was sent to Tangiers to study, a great rarity in her day, but she was a beauty even at a young age and the apple of her father's eye. She yearned to know the world beyond the desert, and her father could not refuse her anything."

Jake nodded as the barkeeper set a tiny cup down in front of him, then demanded, "Why are you telling me this?"

"They met when my father began traveling to Morocco on smuggling runs after the First War," she went on, ignoring his question. "After they married, she returned with him to a little fisherman's cottage by the Bay of Marseille and filled it with books and songs and light and laughter. We learned the English language together, my mother and I. She loved learning for learning's sake. They both died in the first year of this war, when an epidemic swept through the city and there were no medicines." Jasmyn raised her gaze from her own cup. "So we share a sorrow, you and I."

Jake could not believe he was hearing this. "Pierre has been telling the whole city about my folks?"

"No," she replied quietly. "Only his mother."

"You still see his mother?"

"Every week," she replied, her gaze steady. "Sometimes every day."

"This is crazy," Jake muttered. "You ought to be talking with Pierre, not me."

"You know that is not possible," she said, pain blooming in her eyes like dark flowers. "Tell me, Colonel Burnes—"

"Jake."

"Jake, then. How is Pierre?"

His answer was halted by the veil that drew back from her face to reveal a naked, aching hunger. He forced himself to reply, "He misses you."

"Yes? You are sure?"

"It's hard for him to even mention your name." Jake wondered whether it was right for him to be saying this, yet something drew him on. Perhaps just the desperation with which she drank in his words, or perhaps something more. "He says he will never be able to love again."

A single tear escaped the jade-green eye and trickled unnoticed down her cheek. "Another thing which we hold in common," she said, her voice a throaty whisper.

Jake felt seared by the pain he saw and the pain he had seen in his own friend's face. "Why did you do it? Why did you betray him?"

"Betray," she repeated as another tear escaped. "Have you ever faced an impossible choice, Jake?"

"I'm not sure—"

"Have you ever seen the only way to save what is most precious to you is by destroying all that you hold dear?"

"No," Jake said, for some reason shaken to his very core by the fragile power of Jasmyn's words.

"Pray that it never comes, Colonel Jake Burnes. Pray that you are never seared by the flames of impossible choices." Jasmyn rose to her feet by pushing upon the table with both hands. Then she leaned over and spoke intently. "There are others who have been asking about Patrique. Evil men with evil intent. They were among the smugglers. But if you speak with them, take great care."

Jake started to his feet, but was stilled by the motion of one slender hand. He asked, "When was this?"

"Two months ago, and then again the week before last. I know nothing more, except that one man bears a scar from forehead to chin and another is called Jacques. And also that you must watch your back if you search among the smugglers."

She looked down at him a long moment, with a gaze that was tormenting to behold. "Take care of my Pierre," she said quietly, then turned away.

Jake watched her slow passage through the cafe. As she passed each table, many people rose from their seats and gave little half bows in her direction. She walked with head held high, acknowledging none of it. A trio of men at the bar turned and lifted glasses in her direction, murmuring a salute that Jake could not understand. The barkeeper hustled out from his station, wiped hands on his apron, and opened the door with a bow. Jasmyn raised the hood up and over her beautiful face, gently touched the barkeeper's hand, then stepped into the night.

Chapter Five

J ake was already downstairs and seated at the kitchen table when Madame Servais appeared on her way to morning Mass. She smiled and wished him *bonjour,* then placed her hands together and raised them to the side of her face—did he sleep well?

Jake seesawed a hand. Not so well.

Bright, birdlike eyes peered closely, then the old lady spoke the single word, "Jasmyn?"

Reluctantly Jake nodded yes. He remained troubled by their encounter.

"Ah, oui. Jasmyn." She sighed the words, then happened to notice the little volume that Jake half hid with his hands. She peered around his fingers, showed widening eyes, and asked, "La Bible?"

Jake lifted his hands. Although he had discovered no answers to the many questions scurrying about his head, he still found comfort in his morning routine.

They both started at the sound of another tread descending the stairs. Madame Servais motioned with one finger to her lips, shook her head, then pointed to her heart. Jake understood. He should not mention Jasmyn to Pierre's father because of his bad heart.

The look in her dark eyes deepened and she said the

single word, "Pierre." Then she shook her head once more and again pointed to her heart.

Jake sighed agreement as Madame Servais turned to her husband. So many secrets entrusted to him. So many questions without answers.

He exchanged greetings with the old man, then accepted the look of approval when his wife pointed out the small New Testament Jake had been reading. Madame Servais turned back to Jake and motioned an invitation for him to join them for Mass. Jake thought it over and decided to accept. Perhaps the answers would come to him in church.

He was surprised by the number of people entering the church for early Mass. Almost every seat was taken. Jake followed Pierre's parents up to what was undoubtedly their customary pew. People slid over to make room for him, then offered little seated bows of welcome.

The church was built of ancient dressed stone. Small alcoves held narrow stained-glass windows, statues, paintings, and row upon row of candles. The people were of every age and description, from local farmers to stern-faced dignitaries in shiny dark suits. Jake followed their lead, standing and sitting and kneeling, understanding nothing, content to listen as the refrains echoed about his head.

He tried to pray, but the confusion only seemed to grow as he sat isolated by his lack of comprehension. Sally, his own future, his friend's distress, Patrique, Jasmyn, Lilliana's rumors—he did not even know where to begin. He began with a simple prayer for guidance and felt as though the words bounced about his own internal inadequacy. So he stopped praying and sat in silence.

It was not until he was leaving the church that Jake noticed a change. He stepped from the ancient dimness with its cloying scent of incense to be greeted by the sun cresting the buildings across the square. A brilliant ray of light shot over the rooftops and almost blinded him. In that instant came a sense of illumination, of answer. He could not explain why, not even how he could be so sure that here was a message intended for him. But he knew. He was being guided. There was a purpose to it all.

Jake walked back home, slowing his pace to match those of Pierre's parents, and knew peace. He was not alone.

"You say someone approached you last night?"

"Just after I left the restaurant," Jake agreed.

"You're sure you've told me everything they said?"

"I'm sure. It wasn't much."

"Enough," Pierre replied, pedaling alongside Jake on the now-familiar road into Marseille. "It appears, my friend, that one of our little seeds has sprouted."

"You know where to go?"

"The smugglers are a clannish lot," Pierre replied. "They stick to their own cafes, their own streets."

"I had the impression that just about everybody here is on the fiddle."

"There is a difference between a fisherman who smuggled a load of weapons for the Resistance and another who lives from nothing else. Many people barter on the black market, selling chickens they have failed to register or butter from a cow hidden far from home. Such things are a way of life for us now. But with the smugglers it is different. War or no war, shortages or not, they would do nothing else."

"You know them?"

"Not well. I know where to look because my uncle knew them. All fishermen do. And Patrique used them from time to time for smuggling people."

Many of the people they passed were pitifully thin, especially the children. Young people sprouted from old clothes that fit their bodies only because they had not grown out as well as up. The men wore dark suits and hats or berets, the women simple print dresses and coats. All their clothes bore multiple repairs; all were burnished by age and wear.

And yet the people of this town remained erect. Proud. Confident. Determined. Jake wondered if he would have noticed it as strongly had he not just arrived from a defeated nation. Here, unlike Germany, there was no air of pervading dejection. Here there was hope.

They stopped as they crested the final ridge and the sparkling blue of the Mediterranean stretched out before them. Pierre asked, "What did he look like?"

"Who?"

"The man who spoke to you in the night."

"It was a woman," Jake said, wiping his brow as the sun rose higher in a cloudless sky. The previous night's chill had proved as fleeting as a bad dream.

"You're sure?"

"The street was very dark," Jake hedged, wishing he could just speak the truth and get it over with. "But I'm pretty sure. Small, slender, a hood over the face."

Pierre mulled that one over, then decided, "I want to go back there first and ask around. Perhaps someone else saw something more."

Jake shrugged as though it was the least of his concerns. If somebody talked, he would be happy. He hated this subterfuge. "You're the boss."

Pierre grasped his handlebars and pushed off. When Jake was alongside and coasting downhill, Pierre said, "Still I wonder why the woman came to you, and not me."

"Maybe she was afraid," Jake said.

Pierre picked up speed and called out over his shoulder, "Why would any woman be afraid of me?"

As they entered the crowded market area, Jake felt himself lifted and carried along by the general sense of contagious excitement. The air was charged with rediscovery. Still, there were ruins and want and decay and loss. Yet the people seemed to draw hope from this very hopelessness. They were seized by a wild spirit of reconstruction. They were free of the fascists' grip. The blindfold was off. What they saw was painful, yes, but at least they *saw*.

Jake balanced his bicycle outside the cafe and waited by the side wall while Pierre popped into numerous doorways and asked his questions. The cafe's barkeeper came out to clean the two rusted roadside tables and set chairs in place. He ignored Jake completely.

Jake turned his face to the sun. The roofs of the surrounding buildings were steep-pitched and clay-tiled. The walls were mostly of dressed stone. The roads were dusty clay or crumbling asphalt or bricks smoothed to glassy roundness by decades of hard use. Even in the middle of the city, the air was sweet with awakening springtime. The sky was an open, aching blue. Jake could not get enough of the air, the sky, the scent of sea.

Eventually Pierre returned, his face creased with thought. "All right. We leave our bikes here and go on by foot."

"No luck?"

Pierre hesitated. "I have the feeling . . ."

"What?"

Pierre struggled with words that made no sense even to him. "I have the feeling that they are all waiting."

"Who?"

"My friends. The homecoming celebration is over, or so it seems today, and now they are waiting. All of them. Everyone I knew and some I didn't. Watching me and waiting."

"Waiting for what?"

"This is what confuses me most," Pierre replied. "It is as though they think I already know."

"You realize," Jake pointed out, "that what you're saying makes no sense at all."

"They are waiting," Pierre insisted. "I felt it at home this morning as well, but did not think of it at the time. They give me only half a greeting. Half a welcome. The other half they hold in reserve."

Jake thought of the way Jasmyn had been bowed from the cafe the night before and said nothing.

Pierre started forward. "Come. Let us see if the smugglers can make more sense than my friends."

Their way paralleled the harbor. Two streets farther along, the cramped orderliness gave way to ruin. The dwellings had been flattened as with a giant's hand. Streets were buried under a field of rubble. A few chimneys rose in mournful monument to what once was. In the distance, a pair of buildings stood isolated and naked, the only surviving structures in the vast acreage of desolation.

Grimly Pierre surveyed the specter, then said simply, "Le Panier."

Something tugged at Jake, a thought that remained only half-formed. "And you say nobody was hurt when the Nazis did this?"

"A mystery, yes?" Pierre turned and started down the lane bordering the destruction. "I must ask my friends how that came to pass."

The lane meandered along the brink of devastation. The buildings lining its right side looked out over a vast field of dusty stone and sorrow. Pierre stopped in front of a glass door and said, "I wish we were armed."

Jake glanced at the utterly silent glass-fronted shop. Overhead were the vestiges of a name painted long ago, now so covered in dust and time that it was illegible. "We're going in there?"

"We must." Pierre reached for the door. "Full alert, my friend. Watch both our backs."

They entered a narrow cafe, and were enveloped in gloom.

The pair of cramped windows flanking the door were so coated in grime that little light could enter, and the cafe had no other illumination. The patrons stood cloaked in shadows. Jake felt unseen eyes fasten upon him as he stepped through the doorway.

Pierre moved up to the bar and gave a quiet salutation. The barkeeper responded with stony silence. As Jake's eyes adjusted to the poor light, he saw a man slip through a back passage and disappear from sight. His mind shouted a warning.

Pierre seemed utterly unaware of the silent hostility that gripped the room. He leaned against the bar, calmly pointed to a bottle behind the barkeeper's head, and spoke with casual politeness. Jake sidled over to a spot next to the window, from which he could watch the whole room.

The barkeeper lifted down a bottle and poured out a measure. His eyes did not leave Pierre's face. Pierre lifted the glass and offered the blank-faced man a toast. Then he took a sip, set down the glass, and spoke a name.

The silence was taut as a scream.

Pierre took another sip. His hands were as steady as his gaze.

"So, the famous captain finally comes to see his brother's old mate," boomed a guttural voice from down the passage, "and brings an American officer to keep him company."

"Major," Pierre corrected, his eyes still on the barkeeper.

"Captain, major, what is a little more gold braid between friends?" A great mountain of a man appeared in the hallway. He was not simply tall. He was huge in every way. A vast frame was covered in so many layers of fat that he had to turn sideways in order to pass through the doorway. "It is not often that an officer of the law dares enters these portals. Not even one who has a great American hero to guard the exit."

"Colonel Jake Burnes," Pierre murmured, remaining where he was. "May I introduce Abdul Hassad, smuggler king."

"Yes, one who needs no ribbons to gain the fear and respect of his fellowman." The man lumbered across the room to stand alongside Pierre. "By Mohammed's beard, if you did not wear the uniform, I would swear I stood before your brother."

"The same brother who brings me here," Pierre replied.

A slight thrill of movement coursed through the room. Jake watched the room and wished for a gun, a platoon, and another pair of eyes. The huge man's gaze narrowed slightly. "You have news?"

"Rumors only," Pierre replied. "But enough to want to know what you know."

"What I know," Abdul Hassad rumbled. Despite the room's closeness, he wore a voluminous navy duffle coat over shapeless trousers and boots so large that one would have held both of Jake's feet with room to spare. "As you say, rumors only."

"I hear that you know something more," Pierre said.

"You hear?" The deep chuckle carried no mirth. "Then whoever speaks of my affairs has seen his last sunrise."

"Tell me what you know," Pierre said, his voice stony cold.

Dark eyes flickered in the barkeeper's direction, then returned to Pierre. "What I know is yours, Major Servais. For a price."

With subtle ease the barkeeper flicked the towel off his shoulder and began polishing the bar. His other hand drifted down below the counter. Instantly Jake vaulted over the bar and locked one arm about the barkeeper's neck while he seized the unseen hand in an iron grip. The man struggled, but his strength was no match for Jake's. Tables and chairs crashed as men about the room leapt to their feet. Jake squeezed until the man yelped in pain, then wrenched the man's hand out and up, revealing a revolver which was now pointed directly at Abdul Hassad's massive chest.

The huge man barked out a command, and the room froze. Dark eyes held Jake with a baleful glare, and watched as Jake forced the gun out of the barkeeper's grasp and into his own.

Pierre had not moved. He took another sip from his

glass and repeated, "Tell me what you know."

His eyes still flickering from Jake to the gun and back again, the smuggler replied, "Others have been asking questions."

Pierre nodded as though expecting nothing else and said calmly, "Jacques and the scarred man."

Dark eyes blazed with fury. "Tell me who has spoken," Abdul Hassad snarled. "By the Prophet's beard, he will dine upon his own tongue."

"Where were they from?" Pierre demanded. "Morocco?"

Abdul Hassad ground his teeth in silence. The barkeeper tried to struggle, and Jake screwed up his arm lock until the man squealed in pain. The greasy little barkeeper smelled of old sweat and cheap tobacco and new fear. Jake raised the gun until it was focused directly into Abdul Hassad's glowering eyes.

"Marrakesh," the huge man conceded.

Pierre nodded at the news. "Did they speak of a traitor?"

A snarl from across the room was cut off by a roared command from Abdul Hassad. "Get out while your legs can still carry you," he growled at Pierre.

"What about Gibraltar?" Pierre pressed.

"I have said all that is to be said," the huge man muttered.

Pierre glanced toward Jake and motioned his head toward the door. Dragging the barkeeper along with him, Jake circled the bar, the gun never leaving Abdul Hassad's face. Pierre opened the door, waited for Jake to exit, then said to the huge man, "You have been most helpful."

The barkeeper struggled harder when Jake started down the sidewalk without releasing him. Jake tight-

ened the choke hold and picked up the pace. The barkeeper wrapped both hands around Jake's arm and
shuffled along on legs that could scarcely hold him up.
His two-day stubble burned Jake's forearm like sand-
paper.

Pierre stuck his face up close to the man's and
snarled words in French. Then to Jake he said, "Keep
walking toward the harbor."

"No problem," Jake said. "Take the gun, will you?
I'll be able to move faster."

Pierre accepted the gun from Jake's grasp and
snarled something more to the whimpering barkeeper.
Jake asked, "Are they behind us?"

Pierre glanced back. "No. It is not their way. They
will wait until dark and try to strike us in the back."

"Sounds noble." Jake shook the man hard as fingers
tried to pry his arm loose. "Then why are we bothering
with this guy?"

"I want to get him out of sight. Down here."

They turned down a narrow, filth-strewn alley that
emptied directly into the bay. When the water came into
view, the barkeeper wailed and struggled anew.

"Wait," Pierre said. When they stopped he stuck his
face within inches of the barkeeper's and roared. The
man whimpered a reply. Another angry command. The
barkeeper spewed a fear-filled response.

Pierre took a step back, his face filled with cold loath-
ing. "Let him go."

The man dropped to all fours, coughed and rubbed
his neck, then struggled to his feet. With one vengeful
glance back at Jake, he turned and fled down the alley.

"What did you learn?"

"The hunters were indeed here," Pierre replied, his eyes upon the now-empty alley. "They have traveled on to Gibraltar."

Chapter Six

J ake returned to Mass the next morning, trying hard not to hope for a repeat of the previous day's revelation. Still, when he remained untouched by the liturgy, he could not help but feel disappointment.

After the service, Pierre's mother motioned for him to remain behind while her husband exited the church. A familiar figure rose from one of the side alcoves and approached. Despite his surprise, Jake noticed the respectful greetings and formal half bows with which many people greeted Jasmyn. Madame Servais smiled sadly at the dark beauty, patted Jake's arm, and joined her husband outside the church.

Jake followed Jasmyn back to the side alcove. When they were seated and alone, she asked him quietly, "Do you believe in God, Colonel Burnes?"

"That's a strange question to hear in this place," he replied. "And the name is Jake."

"I come here to see Pierre's mother," she said, "and to know a moment's peace. That is such a hard thing to find in my life that I dare not doubt or question or search too deeply."

As gentle as the beat of dove's wings, as powerful as the rain, Jake felt a gift of words descend into his mind and heart. In the instant of receiving, he knew that by sharing the words he could make the Invisible real. "Perhaps if you dared to search and question, the peace would not be so fleeting."

"I see you have answered my question," she said softly.

But the giving was not yet complete. "True peace carries with it the gifts of healing and of forgiveness. Not for an instant, but for a lifetime."

She was silent for a time, then asked, "And what if the forgiveness I seek is not from God? What if I pray to be forgiven by one who can never do so?"

Jake waited, but further words did not come. Instead, his heart filled with a silent compassion. For her, for Pierre, for a world awakening from the tragedy of war. He tried to make the feeling live for her as well by giving words of his own. "Then I will pray for you both."

"I wonder if Pierre understands," she said softly, "just how special a friend you truly are."

To that Jake had no reply.

They sat in shared stillness for a moment until she asked, "I have heard of your conflict with the smugglers yesterday."

"How?"

She waved it aside. "I will speak to friends. Pierre's family will be guarded against attack. Can you tell him that?"

"I don't see how," Jake replied. "Not without telling him about you and—"

She interrupted him with, "What will you do now?"

Jake sighed acceptance of her refusal. "We have heard from the smugglers that the hunters have traveled on to Gibraltar. Pierre wants to leave tonight on the train for Madrid, and travel on from there as swiftly as we can."

She thought for a moment, then decided. "I shall take a compartment well away from yours."

"How?" Jake looked down on her. "From the sound of things, unless you have a military pass, seats on the international trains are booked solid for months."

She rose to her feet. "I have very few contacts in Gibraltar, but perhaps another pair of eyes and ears will be of help. And if your way leads from there to Morocco, I will be able to do more for Pierre."

"You still love him," Jake said quietly.

"Love?" Sorrow filled every pore of her being. "Last night I dreamed of holding his hand once again. I knew contentment for the first time in years. As I sat there, I looked down at the hands in my lap, and I could not tell which fingers were my own."

"Pierre," Jake said, then stopped. He was going to say, Pierre is a lucky guy, but caught himself just in time.

"Pierre," she sighed, and reached out one hand to steady herself upon the back of the pew. "Pierre was more than a part of me. He was all of me."

"Then why—"

"If I hear of something, I will search you out," she said, and raised the hood to veil herself once again. "The shadows have become my friends, Colonel Burnes. There is a chance that I can find what remains hidden to you."

Chapter Seven

Beyond the Cerbère border station, the track changed gauge. All passengers alighted and carried their bags through customs before boarding the Spanish train. The French customs' search was perfunctory. The Spaniards' inspection was anything but. Fascist soldiers in gleaming black leather and funny feathered caps watched over the scowling customs officers. Above them all hung a brooding portrait of General Francisco Franco, undisputed leader of fascist Spain.

The mountainous terrain was far more arid on the Spanish side of the Pyrenees. Beyond Barcelona they entered the vast plains of the Spanish heartland, which baked under a sun already eager for another summer.

At Madrid, before boarding the Gibraltar-bound train, Pierre and Jake scoured the area for food. Like many of the Spanish towns through which their train had passed, Madrid was a patchwork of normalcy and war-torn destruction. For several blocks they saw little indication that the country had recently suffered through a horrific civil war. Then scars emerged, destruction so severe Jake doubted if the country could ever recover.

The streets near the city's central station were so jammed with people it was almost possible for Jake to lift his feet and be carried along. Police and black-belted military were everywhere. The atmosphere was tensely unsettling, yet without any clear indication that anything was wrong. The entire region held a sense of forced gaiety, like the laughter heard at a wake.

There was little automobile traffic. Jake saw a number of army transports, a few ancient cars hung together with rust and baling wire, the occasional overloaded truck, sporadic tired and wheezy buses. But in truth the streets belonged to the pedestrians and the bicyclists and the soldiers.

There was little food to be had until Jake entered an apparently empty store and pulled out American dollars. Then everything was laid out before him—flagons of wine, a huge pie-shaped hunk of cheese, smoked beef, dried tomatoes, the season's first fruits, bread still warm from the oven. What the shopkeeper himself did not have, he scurried out and obtained from his neighbors. Pierre and Jake filled two sacks, in case provisions were scarce in Gibraltar, and hurried back.

As they entered the station, Pierre confessed, "I thought I would be leaving a great burden behind in Marseille, but I find I carry it with me still."

Jake swerved around a porter struggling to maneuver a bulky wheeled wagon through the crowds. "Why's that?"

"I have been so afraid," Pierre said.

The words sounded so alien, coming as they did from Pierre's mouth, that Jake had no idea what to say except, "You?"

"All the while that we were in Marseille. Strange, yes?" Pierre's smile meant nothing. "Every time we went into town, I was filled with terror at the thought that this street, this cafe, this turning, would reveal her."

"Jasmyn," Jake said, hating the subterfuge more than ever. It was there on his tongue to say that she was here, on the train, to push Pierre to go and find her, speak with her, make peace with her. But he could not. Something held him back. Amid the clamor of the Madrid station came a calm understanding that they themselves would have to choose their own time, their own way.

"So often I imagined seeing her," Pierre went on, his eyes pained by the vision of what only he could see. "My mind would become filled with the sight of her, and I would be so terrified I could scarcely go forward. There she would be, walking toward me, looking as only she could look. And the thought alone would be enough to almost shatter my world. Break it into a million pieces that would never fit together ever again."

"You should have sought her out," Jake said quietly.

"You think so?" Pierre turned sorrowful eyes toward him.

"You can't go through the rest of your life like this."

To his surprise, Pierre did not object. Instead, he set down his sack like an old man releasing a too-heavy burden. Slowly he straightened and said, "There was a voice in my heart which said the same. But my mind would scream, what if I did and it destroyed me?"

"It's a risk you need to take," Jake said, wondering at the strength that let him say such things with such confidence.

"You speak as though it is still a possibility," Pierre said. "Do you think I should give up this search for my brother? Return to Marseille and seek her out? Is that what you are saying?"

There in a silent thunderbolt of power came the answer. Unbidden, unexpected, yet in his heart to be spoken, given, shared with one in need. "You don't need to see her to forgive her," Jake replied.

The words seemed to strip Pierre bare. "Forgive," he said.

"It's the only way you will ever leave the burden behind," Jake said, knowing it was the truth, yet wondering still.

"You know what she did," Pierre protested.

"I know," Jake said.

"Then how can you speak of such a thing?"

"Because I want to see you healed," Jake said. "If you punish her, you punish yourself." As suddenly as the power had arrived, it departed, leaving him embarrassed for having spoken at all. He hefted his sack and walked away. "Let's get on board."

Once the train was under way, he left Pierre in their compartment and maneuvered down the jammed hall to the back of the railcar. A narrow door opened onto a gangway connecting to the next car. The passage was metal floored and open to the wind and the heat and the train's rattling roar. Jake stood with two other young men and swayed in rhythm with the train. It was far too noisy for conversation. The engine's smoke blew past in great swirling puffs, except on the slower curves, when it forced its way into the gangway and made breathing difficult. The two other men soon had enough and returned to the train's more protected interior.

Jake stared out over the brilliantly lit Spanish landscape and felt ashamed for having spoken with such authority. Now that it was over, he wondered how he could ever have felt so sure of anything. Especially faith. Even more, how faith could be applied to someone else's problems. First Jasmyn at the church, and now Pierre. Spouting off answers as though he knew everything, even though he had more questions than answers about his own life. Jake stared at the earth rushing by just below his feet and shook his head. It did not make any sense at all.

Words chanted through his brain in time to the train's rhythmic rattle. Sally is gone. Sally is gone. Jake rubbed his face, tried to squeeze silence in through his temples. How could he give advice about relationships when his own love life was in shambles? Sally is gone. Sally is gone. Sally is gone.

Chapter Eight

At the frontier between Spain and Gibraltar, Jake was jerked upright by the sight of an officer in American naval whites passing their compartment. The man was clearly as surprised as Jake to see a fellow American, for he was already out of sight before the facts clicked into place. He backpedaled, inspected Jake with widening eyes, then pushed open the compartment door. "Afternoon, Colonel."

Jake was on his feet. "Commander. Care to join us?"

"Don't mind if I do. Seats are as scarce as hen's teeth on this train." He cast a glance at Jake's medals, then said, "Don't believe I've seen you around here before."

"Official leave. First time in these parts. Like to introduce Major Pierre Servais, commander of the French garrison at Badenburg."

"Major." He nodded toward Pierre, then offered Jake his hand. "Harry Teaves. Adjunct to the supply depot on Gibraltar."

"Jake Burnes. I run the Karlsruhe base."

Commander Teaves seated himself, asked, "So what brings you fellows to Gibraltar?"

Jake cast a glance Pierre's way. The Frenchman's mobile features furrowed momentarily before he gave

Jake a single nod. Jake turned back to Teaves. "It's a long story, Commander. Might take awhile."

"We've got half an hour before we arrive. If the train's on time, which it hasn't been since sometime last century."

Jake recounted their search, beginning with Lilliana's disclosure. Harry Teaves proved to have two of the most expressive eyebrows Jake had ever come across. By the time Jake finished his explanation, the eyebrows had crawled up so high they were almost touching his hairline.

"That's some tale," Commander Teaves said, looking from one to the other. "So you think maybe there are a couple of thugs hunting your brother in Gibraltar?"

"We do not even know if my brother is alive," Pierre replied. "But the barkeeper in Marseille did say they were coming here."

"Got any description?"

"Again, we're not sure, but they might be the same people I was warned against," Jake replied.

"By the woman who just happens to find you in the middle of the night, did I get that one straight?" Teaves shook his head. "Lemme tell you. If you two weren't about the soberest looking officers I'd ever met, with a string of ribbons suggesting you're on the up and up, I'd say it was time to pop you in the loony bin."

"I realize the chances are long," Pierre said. "But I must at least try to check this out."

The commander nodded as he mulled it over, then said to Jake, "Mind if I ask what's in it for you, Colonel?"

"Pierre is a good friend," Jake said, then after a struggle he went on. "I lost my own brother at Normandy. If it was Jeff we were talking about here, I'd travel to hell and back on the breath of a chance."

"Not me," Teaves replied conversationally. "My brother sat out the war in a cushy office, pushing papers for the war effort. We never got along."

"You saw action?" Pierre asked.

"Little bit. Here and there. Joined up in '41. Got to see some too-hot Pacific islands I don't ever want to visit, not ever again." He inspected Pierre. "You?"

"North Africa. Then the push through Belgium."

"Heard it was nip and tuck there for a while."

"As you say," Pierre replied, "I have no desire to retrace my steps."

"What about you, Colonel?"

"The name's Jake. I spent more time than I wanted walking Italian back roads."

"Between the three of us, we've got just about the whole world covered," Teaves said. "Sounds like a pretty good reason to offer my help. That and the fact that you've told me the biggest whopper I've heard since getting assigned to shore duty."

"It's the truth," Pierre declared. "All of it."

"It better be," Teaves said, his tone easy. "One thing I discovered while dodging incoming shells was life's too short to go goose hunting unless there's a goose to be caught."

Even in its tatty post-war state, Gibraltar was a monument to British imperialism. The official buildings were strong and sturdy as the cliffs towering overhead. Porticoes were supported by great pillars atop flights of steps fifty feet wide. Sweeping parade grounds of immaculate green were bordered by flowers and flagpoles. The air was a strange mixture of Spanish spice and British formality. Uniforms were everywhere.

Teaves led them to the main British depot. Beyond endless rows of squat warehouses stretched the combined might of the Allied navy. The war-gray battleships were too numerous to count. Flags fluttered in the strong sea breeze. Klaxons sounded their whoop-whoop in a continual shout of comings and goings. Tugs worked frantically to maneuver the great warships to and from anchor.

He left them at the main gates and returned a quarter hour later to announce, "Admiral Bingham of the Royal Navy wants to check you out."

As they followed him down the rank of weary buildings, Jake asked, "How do we handle it?"

"Straight as an arrow. Bingham is rumored to keep a set of bone-handled skinning knives for people who waste his time. I've been careful not to find out if it's true."

They were ushered into a room dominated by a crusty old warrior with a manner as clipped as his moustache. "Teaves reports you are here on unofficial business."

"Strictly, sir," Jake agreed, remaining at rigid attention.

"May I be so bold as to see your papers?"

Together he and Pierre handed over their leave and travel documents. The admiral inspected them carefully before announcing, "They appear to be in order." He raised his eyes. "Very well. I'm listening."

Jake went through their story much more concisely with the admiral. When he was through, Bingham inspected them thoughtfully for a moment, then declared, "I am in full agreement with Commander Teaves. Yours is an admirable quest. Nasty business, this destruction of families. How can I help?"

Jake was caught flat-footed. "To be honest, sir, I don't have any idea. This was the last thing we expected."

"Well, if something arises, don't hesitate to contact me through Teaves here." He looked at the commander. "I assume you were going to assign them berths."

"With your permission, sir."

"See to it." He turned back to Jake. "The governor is giving a little do this evening. Seven sharp. Did you bring a dress kit?"

"Yessir."

"Bound to be a bit rumpled after your travels. I'll have my aide stop by and give your kit a good pressing and polishing."

"That won't—" Jake was stopped by the commander's discreet cough. He immediately changed tack. "That's most kind, sir. Thank you."

"Right. Until seven then."

When they were back outside, Jake and Pierre released a joint sigh. "I didn't realize what a chance you were taking," Jake said, "bringing us in like that."

"We are in your debt," Pierre agreed.

"Now that's what I like to hear," Teaves said cheerfully. "Nothing like a little gratitude to set the day straight. Let's see you to your quarters, then I'll have to get to work. As you can see, Bingham keeps this place running like a top."

"The whole of Gibraltar is a fortress town," Teaves told them. "Its population has lived under the shadow of attack for over a thousand years."

A gentle spring dusk painted Main Street with swatches of gay pastels. The thoroughfare was crowded with people taking their traditional evening stroll. Jake spotted uniforms from half a dozen different nations.

Commander Teaves kept up a running commentary as they walked toward the Governor's House. Above their heads, the Rock was a timeless gray bastion that dominated the peninsula. Its peak remained enshrouded in a faint veil made multicolored by the setting sun. The high ridge stretched out like the bleached backbone of some great prehistoric beast.

"Gibraltar was one of the two ancient pillars of Hercules," Harry Teaves explained, "and has been fought over since the dawn of history. Whoever controls Gibraltar controls entry into the Mediterranean. Modern Gibraltan history began with its Moorish capture in the eighth century. Since then it has belonged to the Spanish, the Portuguese, and now the British for the past two hundred years."

At the great iron gates flanking the Governor's House, Teaves stopped before two honor guards in burnished helmets and presented their names. "Don't know if you'll find anything of use here," he said, "but contacts like these can never hurt."

"We are truly grateful," Pierre replied solemnly and followed Teaves through the semitropical garden surrounding the palace.

"I'll have to leave you to your own devices for a while," Teaves said as they mounted the great steps. "This is my chance to bend the ear of the ones in power. Come find me if there's anything you need. I'll join you as soon as I can."

The British High Commissioner's residence was a former Franciscan convent. Its formal gardens overlooked a cream-colored palace of Spanish-Moorish design.

Jake and Pierre repeated their names to the major-domo, heard themselves announced as they entered the reception line, and allowed themselves to be passed down from hand to hand. Then they were released into the crowd.

The great reception hall was lit by chandeliers holding hundreds of flickering gas flames. The light was caught and reflected by the medals and gold braid and shining dress scabbards worn by many of the officers, as well as by the king's ransom of jewelry worn by many of the women. Yet no amount of refined dress could mask the fact that most of the people here looked exhausted.

Jake moved from group to group, smiling and bowing and shaking hands. Inwardly he reflected that almost everyone looked as though they had been old all their lives.

"Colonel Burnes," a voice said from beside him, and instinctively Jake stiffened. "Good of you to join us."

"Nice of you to invite us, Admiral Bingham," Jake replied.

"Not at all, not at all." Bingham walked up and said, "Perhaps you would allow me to introduce you to an old friend."

A husky voice behind Jake said, "What an utterly dastardly thing to say about a lady."

Admiral Bingham looked behind Jake and smiled, a feat Jake would not have thought possible. "Now, Millicent, you know exactly what I meant."

"That does not excuse your ill manners." A diminutive woman of extremely advanced years tottered into view and looked up at Jake. "Why is it, sir, that you

Yanks insist on growing your men so overly tall?"

"Colonel Burnes, allow me to present Lady Millicent Haskins, the grande dame of Gibraltar society."

"Nonsense. I am simply an old busybody who does not have the good sense to lie down and give up the ghost, as most people around here wish I would."

"None of that." Admiral Bingham's bark was softened by his second smile of the evening. "We would all be positively lost without you."

"Very well, you are forgiven." She patted the admiral's arm. "Now, run along and let me wring this picture-perfect officer of all his gossip."

Admiral Bingham bowed and spun on his heel. Millicent Haskins then guided Jake toward an empty sofa by the side wall. "I do hope you will permit me to sit down, Colonel. One of the greatest afflictions of old age is the inability to remain comfortable upon my feet for more than a few moments at a time."

"I feel that way already," Jake replied, "and you must have a good ten years on me."

Age-spotted cheeks dimpled with a smile. "Why, how gallant." She eased herself down. "Ah, that is much better. Now then, Colonel. Tell me about this quest of yours."

"It is my friend's really." Swiftly Jake recounted his tale. Then he allowed himself to be taken back through the story in far greater detail.

When he finished to his companion's satisfaction, she was silent a moment, then said, "I am not sure how much I can help you, Colonel. You see, I have only returned here to my homeland three months ago."

"You've been away?"

"We have all been away. In 1940, the entire civilian population of Gibraltar, some thirteen thousand people, was evacuated. The main reason was defense. The Rock was the key to passage into the Mediterranean, you see, and way had to be made for the incoming soldiers.

"First we went to French Morocco, but we were there scarcely a month before France fell. We were then shipped to England. It was only this past winter that we were permitted to return." She looked out over the swirling, sparkling crowd and smiled at the memory. "When the ship neared the strait and we first caught sight of the Rock, the feeling was indescribable. It was a dream come true. I had been so afraid that I would not live to see the day."

"From what I have seen of the place," Jake said, "your home is beautiful."

"Yes, it is. We are dominated by the sea and the mountain and the military. Either you love such an atmosphere or you leave."

"You certainly look at home here." Jake drifted into polite conversation. No matter how charming Lady Haskins might be, she did not appear to be the kind of person with connections to the local underworld.

Shrewd eyes showed awareness of his wandering attention. "Have you wondered, Colonel, why a member of the French Underground would seek to flee to territory firmly in British hands?"

Jake looked back down at the tiny woman and reflected that perhaps Admiral Bingham had been right in bringing them together after all. "No, I hadn't."

"I find that most intriguing." She thought a moment, then said, "Traitor. You are sure he used that word?"

"It's what the girl reported to us. She was absolutely positive about the message."

"Then hard as it may be for your French friend to accept," Millicent Haskins said, turning her bright gaze back toward Jake, "I think it would be wise to consider that the traitor is one of his own countrymen."

"There is much truth in what the old woman has said to you," Pierre said as they made their way back to naval quarters.

"Yeah, Millie Haskins is some lady," Commander Teaves said. "She's got the vision of an eagle. Sees right to the heart of an issue."

"You know her well?" Jake asked.

"Everyone knows Millie. She makes it a point of making everybody's business her own. Sort of considers all who live here as part of her extended family. The locals call her the Matron of Gibraltar."

"I have been troubled by Patrique's travel to Gibraltar without knowing why," Pierre went on. "Now I can see no other reason for it but this one."

Teaves skirted around a pair of quarreling curs. "Any idea who this traitor fellow might be?"

"None." Pierre hesitated, then said, "Perhaps it is because I do not wish to think too deeply."

"May be your only way of finding out who was behind your brother's disappearance," Teaves pointed out.

Jake was beginning to realize that the commander's easygoing voice was a velvet glove cloaking a steel-keen mind. "That makes very good sense."

"Just conjecture, but maybe the way to find your brother, or at least find out what happened to him, is to hunt down the hunters."

"If it was indeed a traitor," Pierre said to the night,

"it would have to be someone who has something to hide *now*."

"I get you," Jake said. "Not something from the war. Nobody is going to chase across the Mediterranean to settle a wartime grudge. Not now."

"Somebody with something to hide," Teaves said. "Something big."

"Or somebody in a big position," Pierre mused.

"A turncoat," Jake suggested. "Played both sides of the fence during the war, and now he wants his secrets to stay good and buried."

From the far side of the road came the faintest of sounds, a gentle snicker of well-oiled metal upon metal. Yet for Jake the almost inaudible noise shouted loud across the years. Without an instant's thought his wartime reflexes had him down and flying with outstretched arms for his friends' legs. *"Down!"*

The wall that was now over their heads erupted with dust from a barrage of bullets. Before the machine gun's roar was silenced, Jake was rolling and crawling for the gutter.

The shadows from across the street emitted a faint curse, then the gunner aimed his weapon lower and traversed a second time. Jake pressed himself to the smelly, slippery stone of the shallow ditch and wished for a weapon of his own.

A shout from farther down the street. A scream from a window above their heads. The sound of running feet. The machine gun made a third swipe at the street fronting the gutter and at the wall above their heads. Dust and rock chips flew in every direction. Then silence.

As the footsteps and yelling approached, Jake risked raising his head. The smell of cordite hung heavy in the air. "Are you all right?"

Pierre rolled over and heaved himself up. "Fine. Commander?"

"All in order," Teaves said, emerging into view. "Other than a little shaken."

"And angry," Pierre added. "I have a distinct dislike for people who shoot in my direction."

Shutters overhead flew back, and a shotgun-bearing moustachioed man scowled down at them. "What's going on here?"

"I wish I knew," Teaves said to the street in general. "Did you see where they went?"

Jake pointed down the alley across from them just as the group of a dozen or so men, some in uniform, came racing up. "I think they were back in there." The men, jabbering in Spanish, turned and chased down the dark alley.

"You gentlemen all right?" demanded the man over their heads.

"Shaken," Jake said.

"And dirty," Teaves said, picking a bit of filth off the front of his dress whites. He glanced Jake's way. "Do you realize you're bleeding?"

Jake swiped at his face, and only when he saw the blood on his hand did he feel the sting. "Must have been hit by a flying rock."

Pierre inspected the cut, decided, "A flesh wound." He stepped back. "That is the second time you've saved my life since all this started."

"You don't say?" Teaves said, joining them. "When was the first?"

"A barkeeper pulled a pistol on me," Pierre replied, his eyes still on Jake. "My friend moved as fast then as now."

The crowd returned, dejected and angry. They exchanged shouted words with the man overhead, who glowered over his shotgun barrels, clearly wishing he could find somebody to shoot. He said to the trio, "They have found shells, nothing more."

"Let me have some," Teaves said. "Bingham will want to see them."

"You have to tell the admiral?" Jake said.

"He'll hear about it all by himself," Teaves replied. "News like this spreads by osmosis."

Someone in the crowd chattered to the man overhead, who translated, "Do you know who it was?"

"Brigands," Teaves replied, his eyes warning Jake.

"We saw nothing," Jake agreed.

The police arrived, took statements. The alley was searched a second time. Nothing. Weary, dirty, and bruised, the three men were finally permitted to return to base.

On their way back, Jake asked Teaves, "Why didn't you want me to say anything to them?"

"Just a hunch," the commander replied. "Thought it might be easier to track those guys if they don't know how much we know."

"The commander is correct." The light of a flickering street gas lamp showed Pierre's expressive face cast in a fierce scowl. "It is time, as you say, to hunt the hunters."

Chapter Nine

"This will not do, mister," Admiral Bingham barked. His anger was fierce enough to blister the air. "I will not permit officers under my command to be shot at!"

"Aye, aye, sir," Harry Teaves replied, his voice as laconic as ever.

Jake, Pierre, and Teaves stood in the center of Bingham's office, while the admiral stalked the floor in front of them, arms locked behind his back. "You say you did not catch sight of the men?"

"We don't even know if it was more than one," Jake replied. "Sir."

"Have a seat, gentlemen." The trio slipped into three high-back chairs. "The bullets tell us nothing, I'm afraid. German make, but they fit any number of weapons. There's a glut of those on the black market just now. Remnants of war and all that."

Bingham stopped before Jake. "That was fast thinking on your part, Colonel."

"More like an automatic reaction, sir."

"Indeed. Your reactions served you well. You saw active duty, I take it."

"Mostly in Italy. But I am stationed in Germany now."

"Yes, so Commander Teaves informed me. Karlsruhe, do I have that right?"

"Yessir."

"I shall inform your superiors of this, Colonel." He resumed his pacing, forming the letter in his mind as he spoke. "They should know that your performance has saved the life of an American officer assigned to my depot."

"Ah—" Jake was stopped before he could start by another of Harry Teaves' throat-clearing exercises. "Thank you, sir."

"Don't mention it." Bingham turned to Pierre. "Would you happen to have a picture of your brother, Major?"

"Yessir. One I borrowed from my parents."

"Let me have it, please."

Pierre unbuttoned his side pocket and drew out a jagged-edged print. The admiral inspected it and gave a start. "I say. Identical twins."

"Yessir."

"Most remarkable. Has it occurred to you, Major, that the assailants might not have been after you at all?"

Pierre opened his mouth, shut it, tried a second time. "Now that you mention it—"

"Indeed." Bingham thrust the photograph at Teaves. "Assign a squad to show this around. They are to take their time, Commander. Stress in the strongest possible terms that they are to visit every bar, every hotel, every boardinghouse, every back-room dive. Ask both after this man, and anyone else who might have been inquiring after him. I want no stone left unturned."

Teaves accepted the picture. "Aye, aye, sir."

"Shoot at one of my officers, will they?" Bingham fumed his way around his desk and back into his seat. "I'll have their guts for garters. All right, gentlemen. Dismissed."

As they left the garrison headquarters, a midshipman approached them. "Commander Teaves?"

"That's me."

"Message for you, sir."

Teaves unfolded the paper, read the few lines, and announced, "We've been summoned, gentlemen. It appears that Millie Haskins has need of our presence. And when that lady speaks, you better answer on the bounce."

The old woman lived in a stout colonial residence, one clearly built with solid confidence that the family would remain there for centuries to come. The house was almost buried under its ballast of bougainvillea. Great clusters of the rich purple flowers grew in such profusion that Jake was on the front stairs before he realized he was entering a deep porch and not the house proper. He spotted a pair of rainbow-tinted hummingbirds feeding delicately from the blossoms, then stooped and stepped into the perfumed shade.

Millicent Haskins sat enthroned on a high-back brocade chair. "Good morning, Commander. Hello, Colonel. So kind of you gentlemen to stop by. I hope I did not pull you away from anything important."

"Not at all, ma'am." Commander Teaves took her hand and bowed stiffly from the waist, but did not quite bring it to his lips. Millicent Haskins accepted the gesture as her due. Afraid that he might do something wrong, Jake simply accepted her hand and said, "I didn't have an opportunity to introduce my friend last night. This is Major Pierre Servais."

"Welcome to my humble abode, Major."

"Enchanté." Pierre bowed over her hand with the polish of a courtier. Millie flashed her eyes in reply, giving Jake the impression that she must have been a beauty in her day.

"Do sit down, gentlemen. Hodgewell, I'm sure the officers would like a glass of fresh lemonade."

"Very good, madam," replied a desiccated butler in formal black.

"And ask Lavinia to join us for a moment."

"Please don't trouble yourself on our account," Harry Teaves said.

"Nonsense. That is the pleasure of having servants. It permits one to go to great bother without rising." She glanced at the bandage on Jake's forehead. "I see you have been injured since our last encounter, Colonel."

"Nothing serious," Jake replied. "We had a little run-in last night."

"So I heard. From the sounds of things, you are all lucky to be alive."

"Luck had nothing to do with it," Teaves replied. "Jake here has the reaction of a leopard."

"You must tell me all about it." She looked over their heads. "Ah, Lavinia, excellent. Gentlemen, may I introduce the finest cook on the peninsula."

They stood and turned and found themselves facing an inscrutable woman of advancing years. Her hands were plump and strong and so chapped they looked bruised. Her steel-gray hair was pulled back into a tight bun. Her face was as chapped and puffy as her hands.

Her eyes were hidden within deep folds, offering only brief glimmers of a shrewd gaze.

"Lavinia has a relative who operates a small restaurant for the locals up near the Rock. Upstairs he has rooms which he rents. He has had a pair of men staying with him now for over three weeks. Tell them what he said to you, please, dear."

"Bad men," Lavinia said, her English heavily accented. "One man has scar." She traced a line down the side of her face from forehead to neck.

Jake and Pierre exchanged glances. "Did they mention a name?"

"No name. But men speak French, little English. No Spanish. Not from here."

Pierre asked, "Why do you say they are bad?"

"Not speak with others. Have much money. Carry knives, maybe guns. Cousin not sure, no saw, smelled grease."

"Oil," Jake corrected quietly, suddenly chilled by the memory of that snickering sound. "Gun oil."

"Yes, so. Cousin know smell. He is hunter."

"You mentioned, did you not," Millicent Haskins pointed out to Jake, "that one of the men you are pursuing has a scar?"

"It's what we were told," Jake said. "We haven't seen either of them."

"Still," Millicent Haskins said, "perhaps it would be something worth investigating. Lavinia would be happy to take you to the establishment, wouldn't you, dear?"

"This is great stuff, Millie," Commander Teaves said, rising to his feet. "If you don't mind, we'll give you a rain check on the drinks."

"I'm sure Hodgewell will recover from the disap-

pointment. Only do stop by and let me know what de-
velops, won't you?"

Despite her age and size, Lavinia set a pace that had
the men scrambling to keep up. As they left Main Street
for smaller byways, Jake asked, "Should we stop off for
reinforcements?"

"Time for that later," Commander Teaves replied.
"Let's check this out for ourselves, make sure there's
something to the rumor."

"No rumor," Lavinia huffed, and picked up the pace
even further. She wore a flat, black reed hat held in place
with a pair of enormous pins. Black lacquered cherries
trembled with each substantial step. She gripped an
enormous shiny black purse with both hands, holding
it defiantly before her body like a battering ram. "No
rumor. Is truth."

Teaves lowered his voice and finished, "Bingham is
not the kind of man you want to bother with too many
false alarms."

Their way took them ever farther from the prosper-
ous central districts. They passed through a market
square fronting two older residential areas. The buildings were seedy and sagging, with rusting ironwork
and facades shedding paint. Yet the brisk sea air and
bright sunlight graced the entire area with a cheerful,
picturesque charm.

People used the most remarkable contraptions as
vehicles. Bicycles had grown homemade side trolleys
and rear carts. Reinforced baby strollers served as all-
purpose carriers. Horse-drawn hay wagons did duty as
city buses.

There were smiles. Hunger, yes. Hardship, certainly. Pain was etched deep into some of the faces. Yet everywhere there were smiles. Jake found himself searching them out, hungering for the sense of being around people who dared to be happy.

Their way took them directly beneath the Rock. The gray behemoth dominated the horizon, rising from rich, verdant growth at its base to stand exposed and proud, splitting the sky, defying the elements as it had through the ages. There at the base, ancient homes bordering the untamed parkland bore evidence of a grander age.

The road took a final sharp turning, from which they could see lines of newer military warehouses flanking what appeared to be a great hole carved into the mountainside.

Lavinia halted just beyond the turning and pointed to one of the old houses. "There. Go there."

Harry Teaves grunted at the sight of a mass of men milling about the dusty front yard. "What is that, our welcoming committee?"

"Don't know. Cousin and friends maybe. You go. I have work." With that Lavinia settled her hat more firmly into place, wheeled about, and stumped off.

"Some of them have clubs," Pierre said doubtfully.

"Maybe there's been some mistake," Jake suggested.

Teaves took a tentative step backward. "Why don't we just—"

But someone in the group spotted them, and with a great shout a number of men peeled off and hustled over. "Too late," Jake said.

A crowd of angry, shouting men raced up and surrounded them. All were hard-faced working people, grizzled and unshaven, with sleeves rolled up to reveal arms knotted from lifetimes of hard work. Most waved clubs overhead. The weapons were long and polished and black and dangerous. The three officers eased into a tight cluster, standing back-to-back, and waited.

A broad little bantam of a man pushed his way through and shouted the crowd to silence. He then turned to the trio, his chest puffed out with importance. "You friends of Señora Haskeens?"

"That depends," Jake replied.

"Yes, yes," Teaves countered energetically. "Bosom buddies. Known her for ages."

"Good. You seek two men, yes?"

"That's right."

The little man spun around. "You come."

Encircled by the group of muttering men, Jake and the others were ushered back to the ancient sagging house. More men massed upon the broad veranda, filled the doorway, spilled up the sweeping interior stairs. Through vast windows, Jake could see that the ground floor was a single open room. Tables and chairs had been plucked aside and heaped in various corners.

The little bantam wore a great fuzz of curling reddish-gray hair that shook about as he cocked his head and announced, "I am Fernando. This my restaurant. Upstairs have rooms. Two men, they stay three, maybe four weeks. You understand?"

"Loud and clear," Teaves replied, giving another glance at the mass of clubs and the angry, eager fists clutching them. "Whatever you say."

The little man shouted and gestured. A canvas sack was passed from hand to hand and deposited at their feet. The sack was covered with dirt and leaves.

"My son find this under my house," Fernando said, his neck growing as red as his hair. He stooped down, released the leather catch. Flinging open the sack, he revealed three machine guns, extra clips, two revolvers, boxes of ammunition, and several sticks of dynamite.

"Bingo," Jake said.

"*My* son find under *my* house," the little man cried, almost dancing with rage.

Teaves had a battle-hard glint in his eyes as he said to Pierre, "Before we turn this over to the authorities, I would imagine you might have a couple of questions you'd like to ask."

"One or two," Pierre growled, his eyes still on the sack.

"Yes, yes," Fernando agreed. "First questions, then police."

"A man after my own heart," Teaves said. "I take it the prey are upstairs."

The little man bobbed affirmative. "Trapped in room. My friends and I, we have plan. You come?"

"No lynching allowed," Teaves warned.

Fernando frowned. "*Qué?*"

"We want to deliver these men to the police intact," Teaves explained. "Not in separate little bits and pieces."

"Yes, yes, understand," the little man said impatiently. "You come?"

They exchanged glances. Jake asked, "What choice do we have?"

"As long as I get my answers," Pierre grated, "I will go to the ends of the earth."

"Not so far," Fernando said, his grin exposing discolored teeth. "Okay, we begin."

A narrow way opened for them through the men thronging the stairs and the second-floor hallway. At the hall's far end a door stood open. Passing through it, they saw more armed men lining the room. Seated on the floor in the center were two very disgruntled men in T-shirts and skivvies. Both men had their wrists and ankles firmly tied.

"Catch while asleep," Fernando announced proudly.

Both men had the leathery complexion of those hardened by long marches under desert skies. Blue eyes attested to non-Arab blood. The younger of the pair bore a knife scar that traced its way from temple to collarbone, just missing the left eye. It gave his fierce expression an even more sinister cast.

The elder was nursing his hands close to his chest. He looked up at the sound of Fernando's words, glanced at the trio filling the doorway, spotted Pierre, and emitted an involuntary gasp.

"It's them," Pierre cried exultantly. "They recognize me."

"Find more guns under beds," Fernando said, pointing to yet another pair of revolvers. "One man try to shoot, but my brother, he move very fast."

A burly man standing over the pair hefted his club and gave them a proud gap-toothed smile.

"Bet that hurt," Jake said conversationally, then turned to Pierre. "You realize these guys are not going to be very helpful."

"With time they will," Pierre replied grimly.

"No time, no time," Fernando said impatiently. "Police must be called, yes? We learn what we need now."

"Just exactly what do you have in mind?" Teaves asked.

"You see." He motioned at the men and spoke a torrent of Spanish. Immediately the room was filled with a hungry roar.

The pair of prisoners showed wide-eyed alarm as arms hefted them aloft and carried them from the room. The noise was picked up by the men crowding the hall and the stairs and the veranda as the procession made its way down and out of the house. The prisoners struggled, but were held fast by more hands than there was flesh to hold.

As Jake was carried along by the fierce horde, he said to Pierre, "I hope they leave enough for you to ask questions to."

From Pierre's other side, Teaves shouted back, "You think you can stop them, be my guest."

The throng made its way around the house and entered the vast, overgrown stretch bordering the Rock. Their own shouts were soon joined by barking cries emitted from the surrounding growth. Jake shot wide questioning eyes to Teaves, who shouted, "Barbary apes. They live here."

For some reason, the chattering screeches raised the crowd's excitement to a fever pitch. The prisoners were hefted up higher, and those arms that could not reach the men lifted a forest of black clubs. A few men slowed and lit fire-blackened lanterns.

A jink in the path revealed a mammoth opening at the base of the Rock. As the men started in, Teaves said, "There are over thirty miles of tunnels carved into the Rock. Hospitals, kitchens, barracks, weapons stores, you name it. There's place here for keeping an army of four thousand men."

The short tunnel emptied into a vast cave. The roof was so high that in the glint of feeble lanterns it was lost to shadows. Stalactites broader than a man hung down in grand natural splendor. The ground was a soft sandy shale, littered with refuse and animal droppings. The odor was fierce.

The men crowded about a pair of metal frames. Jake stepped closer and saw they were white hospital beds, minus their mattresses. The prisoners struggled frantically, but powerful hands held them fast as their ropes were untied. The prisoners were then laced spread-eagled to the bed frames. Each rope was tested carefully a dozen times; then Fernando straightened and motioned. Gradually the hubbub settled into silence. He gestured toward the trio. "You speak now."

Teaves stepped forward. "Do you two understand English?"

There was no reply.

He made a broad gesture, taking in the tightly packed horde of armed and scowling men. "I don't know exactly what they've got in store for you, but I think we can all assume it's not going to be pleasant. So why don't you do us all a favor, answer this man's questions, and we'll ship you off to a nice, safe, comfortable cell."

The scar-faced man spit in Teaves' direction. Pierre stepped forward and barked a command down at the prisoners in French. They glowered and remained silent. Again he tried, and received the same response as Teaves'.

Fernando stepped forward, as puffed-up as an actor on the stage. "Is enough, yes? You wait, we get answers."

"That's very kind of you," Teaves said, showing a moment's squeamishness. "But to be honest, perhaps this is a matter for the police."

"No, no, no police," Fernando said impatiently, pushing the officers back. "Not now. Later, but not now.

Now we get you answers." He grinned fiercely. "And payment for room, yes?"

"I'm not sure I want to watch this," Jake said quietly.

"You go stand there," the little man said, directing them to where many of the others were already headed. "Now."

Reluctantly they allowed themselves to be led into the shadows. As their eyes adjusted, they saw that the other men were climbing up a series of narrow steps and crowding into broad alcoves carved from the walls of the cave. Room was made for them at the front of one alcove. They stood on the edge and looked out to where the two men lay tied. The last man to retreat from the cave floor was Fernando. He took a sack from his brother, then stooped and slid several objects under each bed. Then he ran over and joined the others in the alcoves.

The cave grew quieter still, until the only noise was the squeaking frames as the prisoners tried to free themselves.

Faintly at first, and then more clearly, Jake heard a series of loud, barking cries. Yes, he was certain now. The cries were growing closer, close enough to echo about the vast cave.

The prisoners stopped their struggles for a moment, their faces turned toward the opening through which they had been carried.

Suddenly Fernando's brother came racing into the cave, screaming at the top of his lungs, his eyes almost popping from his skull. In his panic he lost his footing and sprawled face first into the sand. But before he was completely down, his legs were already churning him back upright. Spitting sand and howling with fright, he raced past the beds and out of sight.

Then the first apes appeared.

They loped forward on arms longer than a man's. Their great reddish-blond manes flowed back and forth as they raced into the caves. Their barking cries filled the air as more and more emerged through the tunnel.

The prisoners emitted their first sounds since capture, shouting with fear and struggling madly against the frames.

Their voices rose several octaves as the first apes loped over to stand above them and grin with long, fiercely yellow teeth.

One of the apes grabbed the arm of the younger man. Jake flinched at the sight and saw Pierre blanch as the prisoner screamed with terror. Jake started down, not sure what he could do by himself, but knowing he could not stand and watch this happen. Half a dozen hands grasped and held him. He turned and stopped his struggling. The men surrounding him were grinning. *Grinning.*

The apes circled the pair of beds, barking their great cries and rummaging about, using the frames as jumping platforms. The two prisoners, although hidden from view, were shouting at the top of their voices.

A chuckle rose from several of the men near Jake.

One ape clambered up onto the head-frame, bent his head far over, and barked down at the prisoner. The prisoner replied with a howl of his own. The chuckles took on strength. Pierre looked a question in Jake's direction. He could only shrug in reply.

Someone jabbed Jake in the back. He turned, saw a man gesture with his chin. Go ahead. He caught Pierre with an elbow, said, "Try your questions now."

Pierre shouted something across the floor in French.

A pair of panicked voices screamed back their reply. Pierre turned and nodded.

Immediately several men jumped down, sacks in hand. They called out, raising the sacks as they came into view of the cave floor. Standing well back so that the prisoners could not see, they began scattering objects around one side. Jake craned, made out oranges and apples and bananas. The apes immediately lost interest in the beds and came loping over. The men stood their ground as several of the apes plucked up fruit and then leapt into the men's arms.

Suddenly Fernando was beside them. "Gibraltar apes tame," he explained. "My brother chief keeper. He feed them here. Others help." He grinned proudly. "Was good idea, yes?"

"Outstanding," Teaves said, his voice as shaky as Jake's knees.

"Go," Fernando said. "Ask questions. Men talk now for sure."

Chapter Ten

Admiral Bingham glowered at each man in turn. "I must say that I disapprove strongly of your methods, gentlemen. I condemn them in the sternest possible terms."

"They weren't ours," Pierre replied for them all. "Sir."

"We sort of got swept up in it all," Jake agreed.

"Officers under my command are expected to behave in a gentlemanly fashion at all times," the admiral bristled. "Am I getting through to you?"

"Loud and clear, Admiral."

"Aye, aye, sir."

"Then we won't say anything more about it. Where are the prisoners now, Teaves?"

"In the brig, sir."

"Well separated, I hope."

"Yessir. Saw to it myself."

"Their injuries seen to?"

"They were delivered undamaged, sir. That is, except for chafed wrists and ankles and one pair of rapped knuckles."

The admiral nodded once. "Very well. Tell me what you have learned."

Pierre took a breath. "They assume I am Patrique."

"They do not know your brother has a twin?"

"I did not ask."

"I see." The admiral mulled it over. "Interesting."

"A price has been put on my brother's head. Fifty thousand francs."

Bingham's forehead creased until his eyebrows almost joined. "The price was set in French currency, you say."

"That may not mean anything about where the traitor is from, sir," Teaves offered. "The contract was set in Morocco."

"French-controlled territory. Quite. Very well, proceed."

"They only had two leads," Pierre went on, "Marseille and Gibraltar. They found nothing in Marseille, but it seems they expected that from the instructions they were given. Their orders were to first check Marseille and then to come to Gibraltar and wait."

Steel-gray eyes bore down hard on Pierre. "When were these orders issued?"

"Just over two months ago."

"And that was after your brother was supposed to have died, I take it."

"Yessir. By many months."

"Fascinating." Admiral Bingham leaned back in his chair. "It appears, then, that your search is not entirely in vain."

"My feelings," Pierre replied, "exactly."

"So what do you intend as your next step, Major?"

"The orders were issued by one Ibn Rashid in Marrakesh," Pierre answered. "Does that name mean anything to you?"

The admiral thought it over, decided, "Nothing at all. Teaves?"

"I came up blank as well, sir."

"Colonel Burnes and I have discussed it. We think we should try to find passage to Tangiers, go immediately to Marrakesh, and try to find this Ibn Rashid."

"Take the struggle to the enemy's lair," Bingham said. "A risky business."

"I see no other way."

"No, perhaps not." He turned to Teaves. "What do you think, Commander?"

"Me, sir? I didn't realize I was paid to think."

"Only when so ordered," Bingham replied.

"Well, it seems to me they could use all the help we could give. Passage on one of the regular weekly transports, to begin with. I believe one departs tomorrow."

"See to it."

"Aye, aye, sir. And perhaps you could write your contact in Tangiers. The harbor commander."

"Quite so. Admiral Peltier. Draft a letter. No, belay that. Send an urgent communication, mark it highest priority, requesting that every possible assistance be granted to Major Pierre Servais and Colonel Jake Burnes."

"Aye, sir."

"Supply them with revolvers and ammunition. I will sign the authorization. Can't have them traveling to the back of beyond unarmed. Then issue these gentlemen travel documents and copies of the communiqués. Duplicates in French. To whom it may concern, from the commandant of Gibraltar garrison, you know the proper form."

"Consider it done, sir."

"Thank you, Admiral," Pierre replied quietly.

"Very much," Jake added.

"Don't mention it. Least we can do here. I'll also be sending a note to your commanding officers." A gaze as domineering as a pair of gun barrels swiveled in Jake's direction. "That wouldn't be General Clark in your case, would it, Colonel?"

"Yessir. But it's not necessary—"

"Know him well," Bingham said, overriding his protest. "I'll give him a call. I intend to do the same with your commander, Major. Let them both know personally how impressed I am with your performance here."

A glint of humor returned. "This matter of the apes, however, should perhaps best be held strictly between us, wouldn't you agree?"

The air was as fresh and clear as the sea. Gentle rollers lifted the aging steamer and sent it splashing eagerly on toward a new and unseen shore. Jake stood at the bow, the salt-laden breeze cleansing him of wrong and doubts and regrets. He looked to his right, where the sun descended in a cascading symphony of colors, and thought of Sally. Here, he discovered, such thoughts were possible without pain. Here the sea and the adventures ahead granted him sufficient distance to look at the past few months as though examining the life of another man.

Whatever happened, he realized, it had been her decision. He had done as much as he could to make his feelings known. He hoped that they could be reunited. He prayed for it. He yearned for her look, her voice, her touch. But here and now there was a peace in his heart. He had given it his best. The rest was up to God and

Sally. For the moment, for this glorious moment of limitless horizons, he was able to let go and turn the future over to more capable hands.

He sensed more than saw Pierre move up beside him and grasp the rail as the ship descended easily into the next deep-blue trough. "The skipper says we should be able to spot land just before nightfall."

Jake allowed his thoughts to return earthward, to matters at hand. "You still planning on heading straight to Marrakesh?"

"It seems best. Then the element of surprise may still be with us."

Jake was about to speak further when in the corner of his eye he spotted another figure move hesitantly toward the railing. One cloaked from head to foot in gray folds. Slender and graceful. Jake watched as one delicate hand reached and grasped the rail to his other side.

As smoothly as he could, Jake allowed the next roller to push him back a staggered step. When he returned to the bow rail, it was to Pierre's other side, so that he no longer stood between them. He sidled up close to his friend so that with the next gentle roll Pierre took a step away. Closer toward the cowled figure, whom Pierre had not yet spotted.

Jake held his breath.

An endless moment later, one hesitant hand rose and clutched the hood. Another breathless wait, and the hood was drawn up and away. A breeze caught Jasmyn's dark hair, and flung it up and out like a dark mane. She stood revealed, exposed, trembling.

Pierre raised his eyes from the waters below, cast a half glance toward the figure to his right, and jerked around with a cry of genuine pain.

Jasmyn turned slowly toward him. She stood tall and regal, her eyes wide and defenseless. The wind tossed her hair high enough for the setting sun to shine through and burnish it like a lustrous copper crown.

Jake turned and silently left the bow. As he reached the shelter of the side deck, he thought to himself that there stood the bravest woman he had ever known.

Chapter Eleven

The train rattled so hard that conversation was impossible. The windows had rusted partway open, which meant both the night's chill and the locomotive's smoke billowed through continually. But this was not all bad, as it kept the compartment's stench from overpowering them.

Goats and lambs bleated and roamed the aisles. The five Arabs crammed into the wooden benches alongside Jake and Pierre passed around a hookah stem, while the tall brass pipe stood at their feet, bubbling merrily and sending up great pungent clouds. Every now and then the Arabs huddled together, shouted fierce arguments, then subsided into sullen, smoky silence. The overhead railings were packed with rolled carpets and bulky sacks and chickens that fluttered futilely, their legs fastened to nearby bundles. Pierre ignored it all, his face turned stonily toward the dark window.

Jasmyn was nowhere to be seen.

Jake had waited almost two hours by the boat's starboard railing until his friend had reappeared. Pierre had remained silent ever since, his face clamped down tight. Jake had let him be as the ship pulled into the Tangiers harbor. When the gangplank had been laid in place, the first officers up the walk had called in French for Major Servais. Pierre had roused himself to exchange salutes and to be ushered from the boat.

Jake had struggled to keep up. As he had pushed his way through the throng eager to descend the gangway, Jasmyn had appeared at his elbow. He had shouted over the clamor, "Last I heard, we were planning to head directly for Marrakesh."

She had nodded as though expecting nothing less. "Find Father Mikus. You will be safe there."

Before he could ask more, he had been pushed forward and away from her. The last he had seen of Jasmyn, she had been staring after Pierre, her jade-green eyes soft and aching with unanswered yearning.

Once into the waiting car, Pierre had adamantly refused what Jake assumed was an invitation to return to headquarters. Their guide had finally responded with a Gallic shrug and driven them to the train station. With the aid of two other officers, places had been found for them on the night train south, a feat that to Jake had appeared next to impossible. The entire station had been flooded with humanity and animals, all shouting and struggling for space on the already packed train. The officer had seen Pierre off with another salute and a stream of words that Pierre had accepted with a single nod. Since then, he had not spoken once.

Three hours into their journey, the train pulled onto a siding and stopped. Jake poked his head through the window and saw nothing but stars and desert and a single wood-lined water tower. A team of shouting Arabs struggled to draw a great hose down and over the locomotive's boiler.

Jake drew his head back in to find Pierre staring at him. "You knew, didn't you."

"Yes," Jake said, determined not to flinch, not to lie to his friend.

"And yet you said nothing."

"Jasmyn asked me not to, as did your mother."

The pain-edged gaze drew even tighter. "My mother?"

"She sees Jasmyn every week," Jake said, glad despite Pierre's agony to have this in the open.

The facts somehow did not mesh in Pierre's mind. "My mother?"

"There is something we don't know about Jasmyn," Jake said. He struggled to describe the reaction Jasmyn had received from the cafe patrons and the churchgoers.

Pierre listened with growing confusion. "You must have imagined it."

"Almost every man she passed bowed toward her, Pierre. I was watching. This was not something they did to other women. They treated her with special respect." Jake leaned forward. "You remember telling me about Le Panier? How everyone escaped unharmed before the Nazis destroyed the district?"

Pierre's eyes widened. "You think Jasmyn warned them?"

"Think about it. There's something we're not seeing here. Even you told me that after the welcome was over, people seemed to be watching you and waiting for some reaction."

Pierre shook his head slowly, struggling hard with what his mind could scarcely take in. "She told you this?"

"She's told me nothing. Nothing except that she loves you."

Bitter, time-hardened anger leapt into the Frenchman's features. "She chose a strange way to show this love."

It came to him then. There in the tumult of an ancient Moroccan train, in the middle of a dark and empty desert, Jake felt himself filled with the same comforting wisdom as before.

This time he struggled a moment, afraid to give in. He found himself able to push it away. Yet as he did so, he caught a fleeting glimpse of an aching sorrow, of a chance lost, of a gift refused. So he stopped, and listened to the silent voice, and found the message waiting. Along with the strength to speak. "Did you ask her how it was?"

Pierre waved the air between them, a gesture so weak he could barely raise his hand. "Words."

Words. They rang in his heart with such gentle power that Jake felt his entire being vibrate. He did not need to raise his voice to command, "Tell me what she said, Pierre."

His friend did not have the strength to refuse. Pierre replied in a hoarse whisper, "She claims she was not his mistress."

"I believe her," Jake said firmly. "And I think you should too."

Pierre remained trapped within the shocking anguish of that unexpected encounter. "She claims to have led this Nazi officer on. He sought to impress her with his power by boasting of his knowledge and his position. He seemed to care less for her as a woman than as a prize to be shown about. She allowed him to parade her about the city as his woman, but she says she never . . ." Pierre hung his head, unable to go on.

"It is the truth, Pierre."

Slowly, gradually, as though raised by unseen hands, Pierre's head rose back up to reveal a gaze torn to heart level by doubt and confusion and pain. "How can you say this?"

"I say it because it is the truth," he replied. "I have seen how she loves you."

Pierre shivered under the weight of those words. "But I heard—"

"Listen to your heart," Jake urged quietly. "It will confirm what I am saying. I *know* this, Pierre."

He waited until his friend was focused upon him before saying as forcefully as he could, "Jasmyn loves you too much to lie."

The desert night lay unbroken across the city when the train pulled into Marrakesh. Feeble lanterns glimmered from some hands, and a few flickering headlamps bumped their way down deeply rutted roads. Otherwise the brightest lights were the ones glittering overhead.

The only taxi outside the station was a vintage Model-T flatbed truck. Piles of carpets lined the back, where passengers could sit or sprawl as they chose. Jake and Pierre flung their cases on board while the driver fluttered officiously, proud of his Western patrons. Pierre started off in French, and Jake caught the word *hotel*.

"No hotel," Jake said, pushing himself onto the truck. The carpets were kept soft and well preserved by the dry desert air.

"Where do you expect us to sleep?" Pierre demanded. "Under a date palm?"

"No hotel," Jake repeated, glad to see a spark of the old Pierre surfacing. "What if the Tangiers authorities have passed on information to the wrong people?"

Pierre nodded at the sense of this. "What did you have in mind?"

"I was told to find somebody called Father Mikus."

The taxi driver started to full alert. "Le Pere Mikus. L'homme de Dieu. Oui, oui, je le connais."

Pierre's eyes remained fastened upon Jake. "Jasmyn?"

He shrugged. "Who else?"

"Tell me what she said."

"Only that we would be safe there."

Pierre stared at him a moment longer, then nodded. "We go."

The ride was brief yet exhilarating. Jake saw little of what they passed—shadows upon shadows, starlight etching strange silver forms which he assumed were houses and mosques. The truck bounced and squeaked down empty streets, grinding gears and sending up great oily plumes with the dust. But the chilly air was spiced with the fragrances of the unknown, and every dark corner held the promise of untold mystery. Jake clung to one side post and raised himself to his knees, so that his face was above the cab and exposed to the fresh night breeze. He took great drafts of the cold, dry air and felt that he had never been so alive.

The ancient car chugged to a halt outside a crumbling clay-brick home. The aged structure was set into one corner of a square turned silver and weightless in the moonlight. "Mikus, Mikus ici," the driver cried, climbing from the cab.

As Jake was clambering down, an irascible voice

called out in heavily accented English, "Who dares to disturb the night?"

"Friends," Jake called back.

"I'll be the one to decide that." A burly figure in a full cassock stumped through the gates. He raised his lantern high enough to reveal a heavy-jowled face with bristling eyebrows. As the visitors came into view, gray eyes popped wide open and his free hand reached up to clutch at his chest. "Patrique!"

"No, monsieur," Pierre said. "I am his brother."

The priest squinted and stepped close. He gave Pierre's face a careful inspection in the lantern light. "Incredible," he murmured. "For a moment I thought—"

"Were it only so," Pierre said solemnly.

The priest stepped back and motioned brusquely. "Pay the man and come inside. Quickly now. The night is full of prying eyes."

The priest heard them out in impatient silence. When Pierre faltered, which happened several times, Jake picked up the pace, filled in the gaps, watched his friend with worried eyes. Finally Mikus waved his hand for silence. "Enough, enough. Two people telling the same tale is worse than no tale at all. You are tired, yes? You need a bed, a bath, food? Very well. All else will wait for the dawn. Come along."

The walls were of hard-baked brick, roughly plastered about great half timbers. Threadbare carpets covered the uneven floor. The only light was the priest's flickering lantern, which he held before him as he stumped up two flights of stairs. He flung back a creaking door and motioned them into the low-ceilinged space under the eaves. "Mattresses and blankets there in the corner. The pitcher holds water. Use it with care. Water must be brought from the well at the far end of the square." He motioned for Jake to follow him. "You can come for the food and save me another trip."

As Jake followed the priest back down the stairs, he said, "It is very kind of you to help us."

"I am not the least bit kind," Father Mikus snapped back. "I am disagreeable, and I am impatient. The great Lord above no doubt finds me difficult. But Patrique was a friend, and there are few of those about in this evil time."

The kitchen was a crude brick annex fastened to one wall of the cluttered house. Everything in it was battered and used long beyond its natural life. The grizzled man moved about, setting bread and cheese and olives and dates upon a simple wooden platter. "This water is twice boiled. Drink nothing else."

"Again, thank you," Jake said, taking up the tray.

"Wait." Steel-gray eyes fastened upon him. "What is the matter with your friend?"

"He is troubled," Jake said simply.

"His brother?"

"Not only."

The priest nodded as though satisfied. "It is a troubled world. I myself am from Austria, the land that spawned the evil called Hitler. I stood and watched my beloved land prostrate itself before the monster, and I did the only thing I could: I condemned all who chose to follow him. I barely escaped with my life. Patrique brought me here, arranged for me to take over this work for the local Red Cross. Do you understand what I am saying? Your friend's brother saved my life and then gave me a reason to continue living."

"I understand," Jake said quietly.

"Whatever you need," Father Mikus said. "Whatever I can do. Now go and see to the needs of your friend."

It was not a peaceful night. Jake lay awake in the dark and listened to Pierre toss and turn and heave deep sighs. Finally he asked, "You want to talk about it?"

The silence lasted so long that Jake took it for the answer. But then Pierre said, "I feel as though my mind and my heart are being torn in two."

Jake searched the dark before his eyes, waiting for the sense of being guided toward a response. He sat up, feeling as though something was coming, something greater than either of them, greater than the problem, greater than the very night.

"One side of me yearns to hold her," Pierre moaned. "I feel the need in my very bones. And yet I cannot."

A silent herald called to Jake's heart. All he said was, "You're trapped."

"It is an impossible life. Everywhere I turn I am faced with the daggers of an enigma for which there is no answer. No matter what I do, I am pierced to my very soul." Pierre beat the mattress with a feeble fist. "I cannot go on. This much I know. I cannot live with this. I cannot. I lie in the darkness and know a thousand deaths."

A flame ignited in Jake's heart. A power so vast it filled his being with strength that could not be denied. The instant of its coming lasted less than the span of a heartbeat, yet in that immeasurable moment he saw his own life linked to Infinity. The flame was a gift, one somehow granted through his meager faith and his love for a friend, given so that it might be shared.

"There is an answer," Jake said softly, and in the moment of speaking felt the light of his heart illuminate every shadow.

Pierre responded with a groan of defeat. "Impossible."

"Listen to me, Pierre. The answer is yours for the asking. I *know* this. All you have to do is turn and ask."

The mattress next to his grew still. "What are you saying?"

"You are lost because you insist on going through this alone. But God has an answer for you. There is someone there, waiting for you to open your heart and your mind to Him. I feel this with every fragment of my being, Pierre. He knows your distress and wants to offer you peace. Healing. He waits to offer you *hope*."

The stillness lengthened, then, "You truly believe this?"

"With all my heart."

There was a shifting in the darkness. Then the broken voice of his friend asked, "What must I do?"

"Pray," Jake said. "Ask for His help and guidance. Confess to your own failings. Turn to the Son and ask Him into your life."

A time passed, measured in waiting breaths, before Jake heard shaky murmurs in French. A love so strong it could not be contained filled his heart. A love meant not for him, but for his friend. Jake sat and added his own silent words to those of his friend and felt the freedom of hope fill the night.

Chapter Twelve

The next morning Jake clattered down the stairs to find Father Mikus seated at the rough-hewn table. He sipped from a glass of tea and asked, "How is your friend?"

"Still asleep."

"A good sign. Sit, sit. Do you take tea?"

"If it's not too much trouble."

"All life is trouble in troubled times." The priest rose to his feet, moved to the coal-fired stove, grasped a singed towel, set the blackened pot in place. "You come from Gibraltar, did I understand that much?"

"Yesterday. Then the night train from Tangiers."

"And you found no sign of Patrique?"

"Nothing except the hunters."

"Then I fear the worst." He inspected a glass, decided it was clean enough, dumped in a fingerful of shredded leaves, and added water. "Bread and dates and goat's cheese are all I have to offer."

"That sounds fine. Thank you."

"Patrique told me he was headed for Gibraltar." He sipped noisily. "There he would find safety, he said."

Jake blew upon his glass. "Safety from what?"

"He would not tell me. He said the less I knew the

safer I would remain. Two nights after he vanished the third time—"

"The *third* time?" Pierre appeared in the doorway.

"That is what I said." The priest waved Pierre toward the only other chair. "I suppose you'll be wanting tea as well."

"He can have mine," Jake offered.

"Nonsense. The air is dry, and so the body is fooled, but this desert chill can seep into a man's bones." Mikus hovered over the stove and filled a third glass. He returned to the table, set it in front of Pierre and said, "Twice before, Patrique disappeared, and each time there were rumors of his death. Each time he was brought back by something that troubled him greatly. The third time was to see if word had arrived back from Marseille. He had sent a messenger, he told me, a young girl—"

"Lilliana," Jake offered.

The priest gaped. "You know of her?"

"That is why we came. We told you last night."

"Last night you spoke gibberish. Lilliana is alive?"

"She is in a camp in Badenburg. I have a letter for her parents. She has suffered from a fever but is recovering and soon should be well enough to travel."

But Father Mikus was already on his feet. "Up, up, leave your breakfast. We must hurry."

Pierre protested, "But we have questions—"

"Questions we shall have until the day we die," the priest snapped. "A good family has suffered the agony of the damned. I shall not force them to wait a moment longer for this news."

"I'll go," Jake said, patting his friend on the shoulder as he rose. "You take it easy until we return."

"Just one question," Pierre demanded. "How did Patrique know of this danger?"

"The second and third times he returned and spoke of it, I have no idea. The first time, he knew the same way he learned to escape from Marseille when he did." The priest impatiently reached from the door. "From Jasmyn. Is she not your woman? Do you not hear these things from her?"

The news shook Pierre to his deepest foundations. "Jasmyn?"

Father Mikus loomed large and crooked in the doorway. He turned back to Pierre. "What is this I hear? You do not honor the woman who has twice saved your brother?" Then he gave his head a curt shake. "No, no, that too can wait. This news cannot. Do you have the letter? Good. Then we go."

The priest set a hasty pace across the dusty square. Although the sun had not yet risen high enough to crest the surrounding buildings, already the night's chill was fading. All the buildings Jake could see were alike—low and brick and daubed with yellow clay and roofed with dry thatch. Walls ran around many of them. Portals were arched in the form of the Orient. The doors themselves were thick and studded with iron.

In the square's far corner, beyond the well, stood a squat building with a pole set over its door; from the pole hung a Red Cross flag. As they approached, a gang of young children came squealing into view and danced a joyful racket around Father Mikus. He ignored them completely, and they paid his scowl no mind whatsoever. All of them were barefoot, all wore the simple cloth shift of the desert Arab, all laughed and danced and tried to work eager fingers into the priest's pockets.

"Wait here," he said gruffly to Jake, and disappeared

into the building. The children knew better than to enter with him. They stood around, eyed Jake with shy curiosity, peered through the open door. A moment later Mikus appeared and announced, "Too early. He is still at home. Come."

The children ran and chattered about them as the priest hurried down narrow ways. After several twists and turns Jake was completely and utterly lost. Suddenly their passage opened into a main thoroughfare that ran parallel to a tall city wall. Already the street was busy with vendors and merchants and herdsmen and donkeys piled high with wares.

A hundred meters farther, Mikus bounded up crumbling steps to enter a derelict abode. The filthy entrance hall opened into a broad central courtyard lined with rusting balconies and laundry. Its center boasted a well, a carefully tended patch of green, and three date palms.

Mikus reached the far corner of the courtyard and climbed the wooden staircase in great bounds. He reached the top floor, walked to the first entrance, and pounded on it with his fist.

A moment later a bespectacled man, burdened by the sorrows that lined his face, opened the door. In German he said, "Ah, Mikus. Good. You are just in time for tea."

"I bring news," the grizzled priest replied abruptly, also in German. "May God be praised, your daughter is alive."

A shriek rose from the apartment's depths, and the bespectacled man staggered against the doorpost. Before he could bring himself to speak, a woman appeared, an older image of Lilliana, dark and sharp-featured and beautiful in a tired and world-worn way. She clutched at the priest's frock with desperate fingers. "My baby? Lilliana? Alive?"

Father Mikus motioned toward Jake. "Calm yourself. He has just come from her."

The priest looked surprised when Jake stepped forward and added in German, "Lilliana is alive and well. I spoke with her eight days ago. She has had a fever and is still too weak to travel, but she is recovering."

The woman broke down and wept so hard her legs gave way beneath her. Together the priest and her husband helped her inside the apartment. Jake stood awkwardly in the doorway, fumbled with his cap, and watched as Lilliana's father held and soothed the old woman, ignoring the tears that streamed down his own face.

When a semblance of calm was restored, the husband motioned for Jake to enter and asked quietly, "What can you tell us?"

"Lilliana was arrested in Marseille," Jake replied. "But only for not having papers. She was shipped to a Nazi prison camp and put to work in an armament factory. She stayed there until the Allies liberated her. She recognized my friend Pierre, mistaking him for his brother Patrique."

"The brother of Patrique is here?"

"At my house," Mikus replied. "He has word that Patrique is still alive."

"Perhaps," Jake amended.

"That such a man would send my baby off like that," the woman moaned. "May he roast in hell."

The husband became rigid. "What do you say!"

"That such a man would risk his own life time and time again to save ours," the priest said gravely, "as well as the lives of countless others, may the dear Lord reward him well."

Jake unbuttoned his jacket pocket and extracted Lilliana's letter. "I have brought this from your daughter."

Instantly the woman leapt up, tore the letter from his grasp, ripped it open, scanned the page, and crushed it to her breast. She rocked back and forth, sobbing, "Alive, alive."

Gently the husband reached for the letter, read it, and looked up at a room he did not see. "I must go for her."

"It would be tough but probably not impossible to arrange for you to travel," Jake said. "I can write a couple of letters that might help, but my influence is barely above zero here, and you'd have to expect long delays on the way. Transport is extremely crowded."

"Pay attention, Peter," Father Mikus urged. "Listen to the colonel. This is important."

The bespectacled man struggled to focus. "What do you suggest?"

"We have arranged for her to be issued papers—ID card, travel permits, assistance requests, official passage, the works. All we need is for you to write the Red Cross in Badenburg and confirm where you are. We can even arrange for an escort, with time—an older woman or another family traveling in this direction."

"My wife and I will speak of this," Lilliana's father said in a trembling voice. "We are in your debt for all time."

"Could I ask, did Patrique mention anything to you about a traitor?" Jake asked.

"Not to me," the husband replied. "Three weeks after Lilliana disappeared, Patrique came to us and told us he had news that had to be delivered in person. He said that she had gone to Marseille as his messenger, and had not returned. He feared the worst. My wife," he paused, then went on more quietly, "my wife was hysterical. Lilliana is our only child. She came late in life, after we thought children were denied to us." He looked down at the letter. "All this time I have tried to hope, but it has been hard. So very hard."

Father Mikus patted the man's shoulder. "We will leave you. I shall return later. Arrangements must be made." He stood and motioned Jake from the apartment.

Once they were outside, Mikus said, "They are too distressed to say it, so I shall do it for them. Thank you."

"You are welcome."

"Come." As they made their way back downstairs, Mikus said, "Your German is good, very good."

"Thanks. I was studying it when the war broke out." Jake followed him through the courtyard and back out into the dusty street. There the children gathered, waiting for them.

He watched the priest walk over to a vendor, buy a fistful of sweets for a single copper, and begin distributing them to all the little hands. Somehow he seemed to know when one had already received a sweet, for several times he slapped away an eager palm and directed the candy into another mouth. When all the sweets were gone, he waved impatiently and spoke harsh words in Arabic. The children laughed as though it were part of the game and continued to dance along behind him.

Jake drew up alongside him and asked, "Do you know the name Ibn Rashid?"

"Do not speak those words in public," Mikus snapped. He picked up the pace. "Why do you ask?"

"The assassins we captured in Gibraltar were sent by him."

"Then this is both good and bad news." They turned into narrow passages just as the sun cleared the city wall. Suddenly their entire world became one of brilliant light and impenetrable shadow. "Good because the man whose name you spoke is no fool and would not spend money chasing after one already dead. Bad because he is a jackal, a hyena, a robber of graves, and will do his best to ensure that Patrique's life is as brief as possible."

As they entered the square, Jake found the courage to venture, "May I ask you something?"

"You may ask anything you like. Whether or not I answer is an entirely different matter."

"From time to time people have been coming to me for advice. About spiritual matters. I try to help them. I pray," Jake said, and faltered.

Father Mikus stopped and turned to him. "You are a believer?"

"I try to be. But when I try to help people, I feel . . ." He searched for the word.

"You feel human," the priest said. "You feel trapped within all that is not perfect within yourself. You feel empty."

"That's it," Jake said, glad he had spoken.

"Good," Father Mikus said, turning back around. "Only when we are faced with our own emptiness can we open ourselves fully to be filled by the Spirit." He started forward. "Come, let us get out of this heat."

Jake hustled to keep up with him. "But I feel like there has to be somebody else who would be better—"

"Look around yourself," Father Mikus snapped. "Do you see crowds of perfect people? Do you see a world filled with the Savior's love? Do you find a thousand people calling out to be used by our Lord? No. You find nothing of the sort. You find bitterness and pain and wounded spirits. You find unanswered needs crying out to uncaring hearts."

He stopped once more and fixed his impatient gaze on Jake. "Accept that the Father is calling you, Colonel. Accept that in your imperfections grow the seeds of His divine love. Be content to know that no matter how flawed you may be, no matter how great your failings, the Lord sees in you the *possibility* of perfection. Why? Because you have opened yourself up to be used by Him, the One in whom perfection is complete."

Chapter Thirteen

When they returned to the priest's house, Jake found that Pierre had returned upstairs. Jake sat on the crumbling stoop and watched the day's growing heat gradually beat all life from the dusty square. There was little to be seen beyond a series of tumbledown French colonial structures, a few tired donkeys, and a handful of dusty Arabs intent about their business. Yet he could not get enough of the scene. He sat and watched the day take hold, and decided that he would go exploring on his own if Pierre did not rise soon.

Jake stiffened at the sight of two figures in Western garb crossing the square toward him. As they drew closer, he recognized Lilliana's parents. The mother was carrying a steaming cauldron, her hands protected by layers of padding. Jake hurried over and asked in German, "Can I help you with that?"

"I am sure the good father has shown you as little concern over food as he shows for himself," she replied, ignoring his offer. "So I have brought you some real sustenance."

Father Mikus appeared in the doorway. "You can scarcely afford to share the little you have, Edna."

"Nonsense. This is a time for celebration. Move aside, Father, and see to plates and spoons for these hungry men."

As Edna bustled into the house, her husband stopped in front of Jake and solemnly extended his hand. "I failed even to introduce myself properly. Please forgive my bad manners. I am Peter Goss."

"Nice to meet you. Jake Burnes."

"The honor is mine, I assure you." The handshake was firm, belying the man's frail image. "You cannot imagine what joy you have brought into our lives."

"My husband speaks for both of us." Edna Goss appeared in the doorway, nervously wiping her hands over and over with her cloth. "I wish to apologize for my words about Patrique."

"They were understandable, given the circumstances."

"They were unforgivable," she replied sternly, her hands still busy with their cloth. "Almost as unforgivable as my thoughts."

"Edna," her husband murmured.

"I have raged against Patrique ever since my daughter's disappearance. But in my heart I have always known that the girl probably thrust herself upon him and demanded that he send her."

"Lilliana positively adored the man," Peter Goss added. "She would have done anything for him. Anything."

Pierre appeared behind Frau Goss and asked, "These are the parents of Lilliana?"

The sounds of English words turned both their heads. Peter Goss was the first to see, and gasped at the sight. Frau Goss cried aloud. "You!"

"Allow me to introduce Patrique's brother," Jake said, "Major Pierre Servais."

"I would never have believed it," Peter Goss murmured. "Even seeing it with my own eyes, I still am having difficulty."

Edna Goss had staggered back to be steadied by her husband. "Patrique told us he had a twin, but never would I have imagined the resemblance."

"Forgive me," Pierre said, his German halting. "Do you perhaps speak English or French?"

"Our English is much better," Peter Goss replied for both of them and released his wife to offer one unsteady hand. "It is an honor to meet you, Major."

"Please, call me Pierre." Despite the extra sleep, distress was clearly taking its toll. His skin was drawn taut over his features, and his eyes bore the weight of exhaustion. He bowed toward the mother and said, "You have a most remarkable and brave daughter, madame."

"Thank you," Edna Goss said, finding her voice. "The colonel tells me she was ill."

"Jake," he corrected.

"That is so," Pierre replied. His tone was formal, his bearing rigid, as though holding himself erect by strength of will alone. "But when we left she was recovering nicely. Hopefully by now her strength will be restored."

"You look as though you have been ill yourself," Frau Goss said.

Pierre did not bother to deny it. "In spirit," he replied, his eyes seeking Jake. "Thankfully I have friends who minister to me in my hour of need."

"Enough of this chatter," the priest said crossly, poking his grizzled head out of the doorway. "There is food, and it is hot, and I am hungry. The talk will keep, the food will not. Come and sit."

The Moroccan lamb stew, called tangeen, was delicious. It was cooked in a clay pot, with quarter moons of potatoes set in a rich sauce of meat and pungent spices. Jake took three heaping portions and stopped only when his belly positively refused to accept another bite. "That was wonderful, Frau Goss."

"Indeed, indeed," Father Mikus agreed, his eyes turned owlish from an overstuffing of rich foods. "Your cooking is a blessing, Edna."

"It is the least I could do," she replied, her nervous hands again busy with the cloth in her lap. "After what I said—"

"Enough," the priest said, but without his customary rancor. He switched into German and said, "The good colonel has demonstrated the best kind of forgiveness by forgetting what you have said."

"It is true," Jake agreed.

"If you find Patrique," she said hesitantly, her eyes on her ever-active fingers, "tell him," and here her voice became as downcast as her gaze. "Tell him I forgive him and ask his forgiveness in turn."

"You have it," Jake replied. "If he is half the man I know his brother to be, I am sure he has long since done what you ask."

"Excuse me," Pierre said in English, rising from the listlessness that had held him throughout the meal. "You are speaking of my brother?"

"Only that he is a fine man," Frau Goss replied in her heavily accented English. "Would you tell him that for me, please? That I said he is a good and fine man."

"After you left us this morning," Peter Goss said, picking up for his wife, "I had a thought. There was a very dear friend of Patrique's, the son of friends, people who escaped with us."

"Erich Reich. Of course. I should have thought of that myself," Father Mikus agreed. "He was Patrique's confidant. Erich was not actually connected to the Resistance. He worked in his father's shop. Only Patrique, Peter, and I knew of his true role. We decided it was better that way. You see, many of our funds came from his father's shop."

"He was killed toward the end of the war," Peter Goss said sadly. "Such a waste. There were several uprisings as the Nazis were pulling out of Marrakesh. It appears that Erich was caught in one by accident and shot. Frau Reich died two months later, they say of an illness, but we know it was from grief."

"We understand from Lilliana," Jake said, "that Patrique had come to the office that night because he was supposed to be meeting a messenger. He sent your daughter because no one else was there."

"And because she insisted," Frau Goss said to her lap and shook her head. "I know, I know. I can hear her now. Ach, Lilliana, Lilliana, what you have done."

Peter Goss reached over and patted his wife's hand. Then he said, "Perhaps it would be worthwhile for us to go and speak with Herr Reich, Erich's father."

"I am not sure that would be a good idea," Father Mikus said worriedly. "Anyone who sees Pierre will immediately think it is his brother. And the Kasbah is Ibn Rashid's domain."

"Even more reason to go now." Pierre was immediately on his feet. "We shall take the battle to the lion's lair."

"But without the two of you," Jake said to Peter Goss. "It may be unsafe for you to be seen with Pierre, in case he is mistaken for Patrique by the wrong people."

"It is a good point. I will lead you there myself." Father Mikus raised his hand to still Peter Goss's protest. "You have a daughter to think of now."

Frau Goss asked, "And yourself?"

"I am an old man who has nothing to lose but his troubles." He turned to Pierre. "You should wear something other than your uniforms. The Kasbah has defied control for centuries. It is full of great hatred for all foreign armies."

The city's walls were high and entered through great domed portals. Squadrons of Foreign Legion soldiers stood sullen guard. Through the entry poured a vast rainbow of humanity. They paid the desert dragoons no heed whatsoever.

The Arabs surrounding them wore a variety of robes and headdresses to mark their tribes—multicolored robes with knitted caps for the mountain Berbers; long, embroidered white robes for the city nobility; sky blue for desert Moors. The women sailed by in isolated majesty, some covered from head to foot, others holding a symbolic scarf entwined with two fingers, their beauty as striking as their fierce pride. Seldom would a man risk a glance, no matter how covered or uncovered she might be; to do so invited the vengeance of a jealous guard or tribesman, never far away.

The favorite city transport seemed to be either by foot or by donkey. Arab traders sat with shoulders bowed low, their turbans unwound to veil their face in cooler shadows, their side bags bulging with the day's wares.

"This is the central square," Father Mikus said as he led them through the jostling throngs. "The locals know it as the Place of Heads. Before the French arrived, all public executions took place here. Then the heads were set on stakes as a warning to all who passed."

Jake felt the thrill of stepping into the unknown. "This place is beyond anything I've ever seen before."

"The Moors and Berbers, the first settlers of Marrakesh, were ancient peoples, old as the human race," Father Mikus went on. "Their heritage was mixed and rich with legend. In the twelfth century, these tribes became swept up in the Arabs' tide of conquest. They heard the stories of Mohammed, the prophet of Allah. They were granted the choice of either submitting to Arab rule and accepting Islam, or knowing swift death."

The great Khutubian mosque dominated the Marrakesh cityscape. It was visible from everywhere inside the ancient walled city. Not even the great wall was permitted to rise as high. They passed by a crowd of Arabs washing their hands and faces and feet at a communal trough as part of the ritual required before entering the mosque.

"The conquerors mingled with the local tribes and left behind civilizations which were both Arab and African," Father Mikus went on. "Though their religion became Islam, it was an Islam decorated with countless centuries of legend and superstition and African desert ways."

Water sellers cried their raven calls, their backs bowed by heavy copper urns. They wore broad, fringed hats to keep off flies that gathered at the scent of water.

"Marrakesh means 'the red city.' Under the Moorish

empire, Marrakesh became the foremost city of Africa, the link between the conquered territories of Spain and those in the lands south of the great Sahara. The city and the countryside has changed little from its foundations in the twelfth century until the end of this war. But now Winston Churchill comes here to convalesce, and airplanes have begun linking Marrakesh to such far-flung places as London and New York. The modern world is crowding in. Whispers of change are being heard, at least within the city walls. In the rest of Morocco, time remains frozen as it has been for seven hundred years."

At a second set of older, derelict gates, Father Mikus stopped. "From here on you must take great care. It is doubtful that Ibn Rashid would strike in the light of day, but one can never tell with the likes of him. This is the entrance to the Kasbah, and within these walls the traders are a law unto themselves."

Chaos ruled beyond the ancient portal. The ways grew ever narrower, ever more crowded with camels and donkeys and traders and Arab patrons. Every two or three paces opened a new stall, each staffed by two or more people, all shouting the worth of their wares. They passed down great open halls of copper, of carpets, of spices piled into multicolored mountains. The smells were rich and redolent and as heavy as the heat.

Moorish wood turners fashioned everything from table legs to statues. They spun the wood at a blinding speed, using a one-handed instrument that looked like a clumsy bow. With their free hand they held the cutting instrument, which was set in place through the toes of one foot. Father Mikus told Jake and Pierre that the quality of this work had won fame throughout the world.

The wool market was a separate entity within the Kasbah. Long before the Europeans discovered modern colors, the priest explained, the Moors were exporting their brilliantly dyed wools, fashioned at the wells of Marrakesh. Here the brightly colored strands were looped on poles and hung overhead. Great rainbows of reds and blues and violets and sunburst oranges festooned the passages and transformed the crumbling market buildings. The winding Kasbah paths became tunnels with shadows of gloriously rich hues.

Beyond the wool market, the way became quieter and less crowded. Beggars abounded, their pleas a plaintive chant as constant as the dust. "The gold market," Father Mikus explained. "The beggars become far worse when one departs. Thus it is that few come here unless they intend to buy, and then only with the company of guards."

"Patrique!" The cry was so piercing it shocked the entire venue to stillness. A chubby, gray-haired man wearing a remarkable mixture of Arab djellabah and dark suit coat and vest came bustling up. "Am I dreaming? Can this truly be?"

"Swiftly, inside, all of us," Father Mikus urged, herding them all back down the path and into an open-faced shop lined with wooden-and-glass display boxes. The boxes contained a king's ransom in gold—necklaces, bangles, nose rings, book covers, stamped blocks.

"I regret, monsieur," Pierre replied once they were inside, "that I must disappoint you."

"Herr Reich, this is Major Pierre Servais," Father Mikus said as gently as his rough demeanor allowed. "Patrique's brother. And Colonel Jake Burnes."

The man deflated at the news. "Of course, of course. It would be too much to hope." He fumbled about for chairs and set them in the shop's cramped little center. "Sit, sit, please, you are my guests."

Pierre seated himself, asked, "Then you have heard nothing from my brother?"

"Nothing since, since . . ." Herr Reich allowed the sentence to dissolve into empty space. His words and motions appeared slightly out of focus, as though his hold on reality hung by a slender thread. He blinked and looked about, forcing himself to remember who they were. "You will take tea?"

"Tea we can have anywhere," Father Mikus said, leaning forward. "How are you, old friend?"

"I go through the motions," he replied faintly. "Buy and sell, pretend that it all matters. But there is little left for me now."

"Lilliana is alive," the priest told him. "These men brought word with them."

"Oh, that is good news," Herr Reich said, brightening momentarily. "The Goss family will be delighted."

"You know they have spoken of immigrating to America," Mikus went on. "Perhaps you should think of joining them."

The plump little man hesitated, then shook his head. "My wife and son are buried here. How could I leave them behind?"

"A new life," the priest murmured.

For a moment Herr Reich appeared not to have heard. Then he looked at Pierre and demanded, "You think that your brother might still be alive?"

"A rumor, nothing more," Pierre said, every word an effort. "But we must be sure."

"Yes, of course you must. Patrique was like a second son. He brought me and my family out. He helped me set up this little business. My Erich thought the world of him. I was a jeweler in Frankfurt before the Nazis destroyed our world. I was condemned for the crime of having a Jewish grandmother."

Herr Reich stared at Pierre as he rambled, but clearly was seeing another man. "Patrique was a friend. He was a *mensch*. If you find him, tell him I wait and hope for his return. Tell him all I have is his."

"I will do so," Pierre replied quietly.

When Pierre seemed unable to press the matter home, Jake said, "It appears that a man called Ibn Rashid believes Patrique is alive."

Herr Reich jerked as though struck by an electric current. "You know this for a fact?"

"He sent two assassins first to Marseille and then to Gibraltar hunting for Patrique."

The jeweler became increasingly agitated. "Then there is hope. Real hope. Ibn Rashid is not one to chase after shadows."

"Can you think why he might want Patrique dead?" Jake pressed.

"No, but whatever it is, rest assured that the reason is big. Very big. Ibn Rashid is a power here in the Marrakesh Kasbah. Not even the Nazis were able to dislodge him. They found it better to use him, which strengthened his power even more than before. They say his tentacles reach all the way to Paris."

"Paris," Jake glanced at Pierre, but his friend sat mute and blind to all but his thoughts. He said, "We heard from Lilliana that Patrique had evidence of a traitor."

"Of this I know nothing," Herr Reich said definitely. "But if the traitor was high enough to grant Ibn Rashid protection in the present transition, and if Patrique knew enough to topple the traitor from power, that would certainly be reason for the thief to send his minions hunting."

Jake felt that something was coming within grasp, something that would help unravel the puzzle. "Our trail goes cold here. We heard Patrique was headed for Gibraltar, but it looks like he never arrived. If he had started for Gibraltar and then found his way blocked, could you think of anywhere else he might have gone?"

Herr Reich pondered long and hard, then announced, "Telouet."

"Where is that?"

"A fortress kingdom high in the Atlas mountains. It is older even than Marrakesh, older than the first Moorish Empire. The sultan there holds life-and-death power over the entire central Riff plains. And all highland trade routes traverse the Riff valley, which means tribute must be paid to Sultan Musad al Rasuli. The kingdom's power had waned early in the century, once the Barbary pirates were cleared away and the seas around Tangiers have been made safe for traders. But when the Nazi chokehold became too tight, some of us began shipping in supplies along the ancient Atlas passes."

"Supplies and people both," Mikus added.

"Indeed," the gold merchant affirmed. "Erich and Patrique often spoke of using Telouet as an emergency escape route." Herr Reich shook his head. "I was against it. I have worked with Sultan Musad al Rasuli enough to know him as a man who stays trustworthy only so long as there is more gold to be had."

Jake turned to his friend, but Pierre remained locked within himself. Jake touched Pierre's shoulder and urged, "Did you hear this?"

Pierre roused himself with visible effort. "It appears

that we must go and check out this, this . . ."

"Telouet," Jake supplied impatiently.

"Difficult," Herr Reich said doubtfully.

"Dangerous," Mikus added.

"We must," Pierre said. "Can you help?"

"There is a Berber supply caravan leaving at dawn to cross the mountains," Reich said. "I know because they are delivering what I hope will be my final request for supplies. The French are still not in full control of the harbors, and shipment of anything except emergency goods remains sporadic, so I must transport overland. But the tribute I must pay, as well as the payments to the tribal chieftains who bring in my goods—" He shook his head. "Together it is almost as much as the goods themselves. I hope this will be the last time. As I do with every shipment."

"Will they take us with them?" Jake pressed.

"If there is a reason." Herr Reich pondered a moment, then brightened. "What do you know about automobiles?"

"Excellent," Father Mikus muttered. "A splendid idea."

"You mean, as in repairing?" Jake shrugged. "As much as the next guy, I guess." He looked at Pierre, willing his friend to hold the world in focus. "What about you?"

"Some. Before the war I enjoyed tinkering about."

"The sultan has a fleet of Rolls Royces," said Herr Reich. "Four, to be exact. None of them run."

"You're kidding."

"It is a story that has been told in the lowlands for years," Father Mikus replied, "as an example of the sort of man who rules the Riff highlands. Once his stables held only horses. Then in the thirties he took delivery of four Rolls Royce automobiles. Thirty men lost their lives widening the highland trails to deliver them, and still they were unable to drive across the steepest slopes—they were pulled by teams of horses and slaves."

"Slavery's been outlawed," Jake pointed out.

Reich cast him a sardonic glance, then continued. "Gasoline had to be brought by donkey over the mountains. As long as the cars ran, the sultan could only drive up and down the Riff plains; beyond that the roads were not extended. But when war broke out, the sultan's mechanic ran away to join up, and now the cars no longer run. I know this for a fact because the Berbers are taking back spare parts, and they joke about it because there is no one to replace them or even to say whether they are the correct pieces."

Jake turned to Pierre and demanded, "So what do we do?"

"Do?" Pierre rose slowly to his feet. "As Herr Reich has said, we go through the motions. We continue the search."

"The Berber tribesmen will leave with the sun," Herr Reich offered, rising with them. "I will arrange for them to come by Father Mikus' house to fetch you and will pay for your passage. I shall call it a further token of my esteem for the great sultan."

"Thank you," Pierre managed.

"It is I who offers thanks," Herr Reich replied. "Even this talk has done my spirit a world of good. And if ever you find Patrique, remember my words to him. All I have is his."

Chapter Fourteen

Pierre retreated back into himself and refused even to speak with the others for the remainder of the day. That evening he retired to his mattress immediately after dinner and did not respond when Jake spoke his name.

Jake was awakened before dawn by faint sounds echoing outside the priest's hovel. "Pierre?"

"Yes?"

"I hear horses," he said, fumbling in the dark for his clothes. "Hurry."

As Jake dressed and threw his belongings into his satchel, Father Mikus appeared in the doorway bearing an oil lamp. "Ah, you're awake. Good. A rider has appeared with your horses. You are expected at the main gates at dawn." He set down the lantern and turned away. "I will see to your breakfast."

Jake asked Pierre, "Can you ride a horse?"

"As well as I can repair an engine. I would sometimes ride the salt plains with Patrique. And you?"

"I learned in the Poconos. They're mountains back home." Jake grinned as he buckled his bag. "It seems like another lifetime."

"Everything that came before the war is from a different life," Pierre replied.

"How do you feel?"

"Bruised, battered, and horribly confused," Pierre said, not looking Jake's way.

"Don't you think—"

Pierre raised his hand. "I think too much. Night after night I rack my brains. Day after day I search my mind. All it has done is to lead me in hopeless circles."

He snapped the satchel's catches and straightened. "So I try to do as you say. At night I talk to the stars and in the day I plead with the dust. I try to listen to the infinite. I struggle to see the invisible. And all it has left me is more empty than I have ever been in my life. Empty and lost and without hope." Pierre turned and left the room.

Jake sat by his mattress, waiting for guidance. He heard nothing, felt nothing save an aching worry for his friend. Then he sighed his way to his feet, grasped his satchel, and followed Pierre downstairs.

The Beshaw Berbers spoke only Arabic and their local dialect, so Jake and Pierre journeyed in silence once Father Mikus saw them off at the gate. Jake did not mind, nor was he troubled by the dark-eyed stares sent his way. He was among an unknown folk, journeying into lands where legends were born. Not even Pierre's morose silence could still the humming excitement that coursed through Jake's veins.

Farewells with Father Mikus had been awkward. Pierre barely roused from his reverie long enough to offer thanks. Jake had taken it upon himself to pull the priest aside and ask, "Can you tell me anything about what's up ahead?"

Father Mikus thought a moment, then replied, "Morocco became a protectorate of France in 1912, but this has had little effect outside the major cities." He stretched out one hand toward where the mountains rose, pink and glorious in the distance. "In the lands beyond the hills, time is measured by centuries and not by days. The French will come and go and be granted little more than a sentence in the tales of tribal life."

Mikus called to where the tribesmen waited patiently. They responded with a few words. "You should arrive late tomorrow," he told Jake. "They will take you straight into the mountains. You must cross the Tizian-Tischka Pass, then enter the highland plains. This will take you to Telouet."

"You know the way?"

"I have been there. Twice. But one could spend a thousand lifetimes in those hills and not know them."

Jake felt the rising thrill of adventure. "If Jasmyn shows up—"

"Jasmyn?" the priest cried. "She is here?"

"She may be," Jake hedged. "She was with us, sort of, as far as Tangiers."

"Sort of?"

Jake glanced toward Pierre. "There are problems."

"Ah." The priest's jowls shook as he gave a jerky nod. "Now all is made clear. But how will I know her? I have never seen the woman before."

"If it's her, you'll know," Jake said definitely. "Tell her where we've gone, and why."

"Very well." The priest offered a gnarled hand. "Go with God, Colonel Burnes."

"Thanks. I appreciate your help. And advice. We both do."

"Find Patrique. Tell him his friends await his return." He gave Pierre a searching look. "And see to the needs of your friend."

The mountain tribesmen rode gleaming steeds which handled the rocky terrain with sure-footed strength. Their stout saddles rose high in front and back. Saddle blankets bore the markings of the Beshaw tribe, three stripes interwoven with the mark of Allah.

The hard-faced men all wore white voluminous trousers and high boots as supple as the ammunition belts that crossed their chests. Their turbans were of dark blue, and matching robes hung about their necks— there to be wrapped about in strong winds and morning chills or flung aside in heat.

Their rifles were ancient to Jake's eyes, a museum of armaments from other eras. Most were single-fire weapons with stocks layered in filigreed silver and barrels as long as a man was tall. But the men carried them with the ease of those long accustomed to bearing arms, and gave little notice to their great weight.

They followed the path of a wandering stream out of town and up toward the mountains. Wild scrub fought for place with the towering palms. The air was sweet with the scent of endless spices and blooming flowers.

Morocco was indeed a land of contrasts. Wherever there was water and arable land, life bloomed in profusion. Where water was absent, rock and shale and sand dominated, and the land was dry and dead as old bones. The distance between these two contrasting lands was often less than a hundred meters.

The mountains garnered rainfall from clouds grown full in the tropical south, so even the dry reaches of their early journey held many oases, with calm waters surrounded by palms and Berbers and camel herds. Water dictated where life could flourish. The villages they passed bordered either oases or rivers. The houses were made of the region's red clay.

By midday the first rise was behind them, and Jake's legs and seat were rubbed raw. His lower back burned from the unaccustomed motion. But he strove to keep his discomfort from his face, and concentrated upon the wonders about them.

After they had crested the first rise, the road became rougher, the air dryer. The lowland's bright, leafy greenness gave way to scrub and stubborn fir trees stunted by trying to grow in meager soil.

The path was little more than a flattened trail up the rocky scree. The horses, mountain born and bred, found footing with the ease of mountain goats. The higher they climbed, the colder it became.

They camped for the night just below the snow line. While the tribesmen made camp and prepared their meal, Jake eased bruised muscles and looked out over a sunset-lit vista of gold and russet hues. The great plains of western Morocco stretched all the way to the sea, while to either side of him rose the jagged Atlas peaks in all their glory. The view added spice to an otherwise unappealing meal of dried lamb strips and corn gruel, and made Pierre's morose silence much more bearable.

As the camp settled for the night, Jake lay beneath his saddle blanket, watched the stars circle just out of

reach, and thought of his silent friend lying there beside
him. The wind spoke to him then, and the clarity of the
night sky helped him see and understand.

Pierre had spent the years of war conditioning himself to revile Jasmyn. All that bitterness, all that raging
fury had carried him through the dregs of war-torn Europe and kept him alive when many other good men
had passed over. Now Pierre's world, bitter as it might
be, was being torn asunder. And his best friend responded by saying that help could come only from a
God in whom Pierre did not believe. Jake lay still and
felt the cold pinch at his face, and did the only thing he
could think of to help his friend. He prayed.

Frost whitened their blankets when the travelers
awoke the next morning. With a minimum of discus-
sion, camp was broken, horses packed and mounted.
The trip resumed.

The pass was recognizable as such only because the
ridge they crossed was three thousand feet and more
below the surrounding peaks. But there was no path
over the saddle of ice and snow, and the wind howled
with fierce fury as the men dismounted and walked the
horses up and over the steep ridge. Twice during their
passage, heavily laden packhorses broke through the
permanent ice coating and sank to their chests in the
deep snow. Each time the entire tribe jumped into action, shouting and heaving with all their might, struggling to free the animals before they disappeared completely into the ancient snows.

On the pass's other side, going was faster but
equally dangerous. A misstep meant a slide down ice-
bound slopes with nothing to stop the plummet for a
thousand feet. By the time the snows began to give out,
Jake's legs were trembling from the strain and the fear.

When they were safely beyond the snow line, the horses were hobbled and fitted with feed bags. Tea was brewed and served with chunks of sticky-sweet cakes made from layer after layer of paper-thin pastry, filled with crushed nuts and lathered with honey. Jake felt his tired body soak in the energy from the provisions, and again he found himself able to look at the surrounding vista with interest.

The road to Telouet descended before them into a wide, flat highland plain. Most of the valley floor was dry and void of life. The road was the same hard-packed scrabble as had borne the feet of Roman legions two thousand years earlier. Through the highland valley's heart flowed a river, which from Jake's lofty perspective appeared as a silver ribbon lined on both banks by broad stretches of green. Along the river's path rose a city as yellow as the barren earth that stretched out beyond the water's reach.

Although in the dry highlands air the city seemed close enough to touch, still it took them three long hours to work their way down the steep-sided hill to the point where the path broadened into the ceremonial road of packed shale. As soon as the horses touched the road, the tribesmen raised their rifles and fired a volley into the air. Jake guessed the time-honored custom had two purposes. First, it announced their approach loudly and long in advance. Second, for the single-fire weapons of old, the volley cleared the guns' chambers.

The city hid behind the tall, sturdy walls of a medieval fortress. Only the great dome of a palace and the tower of a mosque were high enough to be seen as they approached. The portals of the keep were fifty feet tall, curved and peaked at their summit, and fashioned from thick oaken planks studded with iron crossbars. A score of turbaned men with scimitars and well-oiled rifles guarded the approach.

When the Berbers were within hailing distance, the chief separated himself, trotted forward, slid from his horse, and greeted the captain of the guard with a bow. Three fingers of his right hand touched heart and lips and forehead. The guard captain responded in kind. They spoke for a long time while Jake tried to match the tribesmen's silent patience. Pierre seemed oblivious to his surroundings.

Jake stiffened as attention of the entire guard party swung toward them. The captain examined him with an impenetrable gaze, then turned and barked an order. His subordinate scurried away. There followed a long and careful scrutiny of the cargo. Each packhorse in turn had its leather covering slung aside. Some carried delicacies—small eggs of pastel blue, salted fish wrapped in seaweed, fine fruit, fresh spices. But most carried metal components clearly meant for machinery. Jake looked at one horse bearing a pair of mufflers and three tires, and understood why the animal had broken through the packed ice.

A pair of guards came hustling through the portals, trying to keep up with a diminutive official. Jake sucked in his cheeks to hide a smile. He knew that kind of man. General staffer, his sort was called in the army, a man who loved giving orders and fled at the first sign of a fight. This particular one was extremely proud of his ill-fitting Western suit and tie and Brylcreamed hair. His manner was officious and bossy and superior.

Experience had taught Jake that the best way to deal with such a man was by meeting him head on. As the official bustled toward him, Jake slid from his saddle, came to bristling attention, and snapped off a parade-ground salute. "Jake Burnes, formerly of the United States Army, at your service, sir!"

The action generated the desired response. The little man ground to a halt, faltered, then drew himself up and sniffed, "Is true, you are mechanic for Rolls Royce motor vehicles?"

"Yessir!" In the corner of his eye Jake caught Pierre swiveling and giving him a questioning gaze. He willed his friend to remain silent. "My assistant and I, we have positively years of experience with motor cars of all shapes and sizes, sir!"

The power of Jake's voice drove the official back a step. "I am Hareesh Yohari. Official assistant to great Sultan Musad al Rasuli, ruler of all Riff." He had to cock his head back to a ridiculous angle in order to sniff down at Jake. "Sultan orders you to fix motor vehicles. How long it take?"

"Hard to tell until we check them over, Lord Hareesh, sir!"

Being accorded a title consistent with his over-inflated ego helped puff out the official's chest and ease his concern over admitting strangers into the palace keep. Hareesh cocked his head back even farther so as to inspect Pierre, who eyed the scene from the safety of his horse. "You, why you not standing and giving proper greetings to sultan's official assistant?"

"My assistant has been ill, and the trip has tired him out, sir!" Jake answered for him.

"Better not illness to slow down repair of motor vehicles," Hareesh warned. "Sultan not patient man."

"Oh no, sir! We'll be starting on repairs this very day, sir!"

The official sniffed and turned away in dismissal. He snapped out orders, and the guards waved the company through. The tribesmen watched Jake snap off a second salute, then heave himself back into the saddle. Once they were through the massive portals, several turned toward Jake, gave him ridiculous parodies of salutes, shouted nonsense in Arabic, then howled their mirth. Jake shared a smile. Officials were the same the whole world over.

He walked his horse alongside Pierre's and tried hard not to gape. The city was as ancient as time and mysterious as the desert mountains that enclosed it. Crowds of people stopped and pointed up at them; clearly few had seen a white man before. Jake smiled and touched his forehead in greeting and received gap-toothed grins in return.

The streets teemed with raucous Arab life. Berbers fresh from the empty reaches strode with confidence down the packed market ways. Their eyes held the far-seeing gaze of those used to desert distances. Princes with eunuchs in cautious attendance stepped casually from stall to stall, the gold and jewels woven into their robes glittering in the harsh sunlight. Snake charmers and water sellers and musicians and acrobats and sto-rytellers vied for attention in the crowded ways.

Doors to the imposing structures they passed were all tall and domed, meant to be opened fully only for riders mounted upon proud Arabian steeds. Set in their middle were smaller doors for foot traffic. And in the center of these were hand-sized openings with stout iron grillwork, through which guards scowled fiercely at all who sought entry.

The tribesman nearest Jake noted his excited gaze, smiled with pride at the stranger's interest in the man's homeland, and pointed up ahead. Jake heard strange calls and cries, and craned in his saddle. Their way opened into a tightly packed square, and suddenly he was riding through an outdoor aviary. Birds of every size and description stood upon wooden crooks or fluttered inside hand-woven reed cages. Their plumage was a blurred riot of color. Their calls and shrill songs echoed back from the surrounding walls in never-ending symphony. Jake laughed his delight and was rewarded with a clap on the shoulder from the closest tribesman.

They were stopped a second time at the portals to the inner keep, and held until the little official appeared. When Jake slid from the saddle, the tribesmen were ready and kept straight faces only by tugging fiercely on their beards. The official puffed out his chest and motioned for Jake to move up beside him. Jake handed his reins to a tribesman and stepped to the head of the procession. They walked past scowling guards and entered the palace grounds.

The road changed instantly from dusty stone to polished, close-fitting brick. They circled a third wall, over which peeked the heads of tall date palms.

"The sultan will personally wish to ask when Rolls Royce motor vehicles ready," Hareesh warned. "Best you know when he ask."

"Tomorrow, sir!" Jake said, keeping to a quick-step march and ignoring the suppressed chuckles behind him. "We'll know by tomorrow, definitely!"

Hareesh sniffed his acceptance, passed under a tall portico, and entered a cobblestone yard lined by servants' quarters and fronting a long line of stables. A large well dominated the center of the yard. "Rolls Royce motor vehicles in four left stalls. You to make most careful inspections, yes?"

"We inspect, sir!"

The official bristled at the sound of mirth behind him, wheeled about, and was met with stony expressions. He turned back and cocked his head suspiciously, but Jake responded only with the blank stare of one long trained in dealing with officers who led from the rear. Another sniff, then, "You sleep with cars. I order food."

"Very good, sir!" Jake snapped off his salute, then went back to his steed, untied his satchel, accepted the handshake and salutations of the tribesmen, and motioned for Pierre to join him. Together they crossed the yard, the tribesmen calling farewells behind them.

The stable doors at first refused to give. Jake had to borrow a guard's rifle and bang long and hard on the rusty hinges before they were able to swing the heavy door wide. Clearly no one had entered these stables in years.

They set down their satchels in one corner and together drew back the dust cover from the first vehicle. The sight was enough even to raise Pierre from his stupor.

The great gleaming hood appeared to go on for miles. A pair of burnished headlights as big as soup tureens flanked the massive chrome grillwork, which was crowned by the silver angel with swept-back wings. Huge fenders curved over the front tires swept down and flattened to become chrome-plated running boards. The driver's compartment had a roll-back leather roof that was cracked along the seams, as was the seat. Yet the damage was nowhere near what could have been expected. The dry desert air had held deterioration to a minimum.

Jake opened the carriage-type door to the back compartment. The musty air was redolent of saddle leather and luxury. Elegant seats faced a bar of crystal and chrome and walnut burl. A swivel writing desk contained a silver-plated inkwell, leather writing postern, and two gold pens in tortoiseshell holders.

Jake looked back to where his friend was unfastening the engine cowling. "All the comforts of home."

"Come take a look at this."

The engine was a straight-eight and appeared to be about fifty yards long. It looked as clean as it had when rolling off the assembly line fifteen years earlier. Jake declared, "You could eat your dinner off this thing."

"Nothing looks wrong with this," Pierre agreed. "Nothing at all."

Jake looked at his friend. "You ready to rejoin the land of the living?"

Pierre kept his eyes on the motor. "We need to talk."

"Anytime," Jake said quietly. "I've been waiting—"

"Ah, gentlemens already at work, is most excellent." Hareesh bounded into the stable. "Is everything you require?"

"We could use some tools, sir!" Jake said, coming to rigid attention. He found extraordinary pleasure in seeing Pierre snap to alongside him.

"Tools are many, on wall in next stable. And equipments. We have much equipments." He motioned imperiously to a guard, who turned and barked a command. A line of servants began parading in, depositing the tribesmen's cargo on the car's other side. "Is good, yes?"

"We should have enough for the job, yessir," Jake said, eyeing the heap, wondering if any of the pieces would actually fit a Rolls.

Pierre heaved a silent sigh when one of the porters dumped a pair of batteries at their feet. Hareesh

squinted up at him and demanded, "Assistant is faint-
ing now?"

"He'll be fine, sir, just give him a couple of days."

"No have days. Day. One. Tomorrow sultan will ask
how long to repair motor vehicles. You will tell, yes?"

"We'll do our best, sir."

"No best. You do. Sultan want Rolls Royce motor
vehicles for to drive, not keep in stables." Hareesh spun
on his heel and departed, flinging over his shoulder,
"Servant bring food. Sick man eat much, feel better,
work hard."

When the livery was again empty, Jake ducked inside the driver's cab, inspected the controls, and announced, "This car has been driven a grand total of
three hundred and thirty-seven miles."

"My guess is that all it needs is an oil change, new
tires, and a charged battery," Pierre said, his head deep
inside the cowling.

"Can't make this look too easy," Jake warned.

"Go see what kind of tools they have," Pierre said,
"and don't try to teach a Marseille boy how to work a
scam."

Chapter Fifteen

At dusk the city sang its throbbing beat. The air cooled, the dust settled, the sun descended. During their meal Jake tried to urge Pierre into talking, but his friend would say no more than that he was not yet ready to find the words. Afterward Pierre curled himself into blankets on the backseat of one Rolls, and Jake set off alone to enjoy the dying day's cooler hours.

The guards by the inner keep's portals eyed him with stony silence as he walked by, but did not attempt to stop him. Jake could feel their eyes remain on him up to the next corner. Beyond the turning, however, he was able to give himself to the sheer joy of exploration.

The city's narrow ways and cobblestone squares were a distillation of the entire desert nation. Members of virtually every tribe wandered its dusty courses. Porters streamed by under the watchful eyes of guards armed with great long rifles and viciously curved scimitars. Traders hawked everything from beads to camels. Painted ladies wore veils which fell away in indiscreet folds. A bearded giant, carrying a full-grown sheep across his shoulders, passed him. A native child drove a herd of goats down the lane, then paused to gaze up in astonishment at Jake's blue eyes.

Desert folk shielded themselves against the growing evening chill with hooded djellabah of soft goat's wool. No man's head was uncovered. Turbans of white or checkered cloth, peaked hats, knitted caps—all denoted tribe and region as clearly as did robes and speech.

Women of the orthodox tribes were dressed in either all white or all black, their faces covered by embroidered shawls with rectangular slits for vision. No part of their bodies was permitted to be exposed, not even their hands, which were kept hidden within the flowing folds. Other women walked with no head covering at all save for sheer silk kerchiefs. Cascading gold bracelets on their ankles and wrists marked a cheerful tune with each step.

Jake climbed the outer ramparts of the city walls just in time to see the sun's final rays transform distant snow-capped peaks to bastions of molten gold. Guards standing duty along the wall glowered in his direction, but made no move. Clearly word had spread of the strangers who were there as guests of the sultan.

A cannon boomed from somewhere down the ramparts. As the echo rumbled like thunder through the valley, Jake watched the city's great outer doors draw shut. They rolled on ancient stone wheels, each pushed by six men, while another six heaved on a rope as thick as a man's thigh. As the doors rumbled closed, the muezzin's call rose from the mosque's minaret.

Jake looked out over a desert landscape gradually disappearing into a sea of blackness. Tiny orange fires shone from tribal campsites like mirrors of the stars appearing overhead. He watched the night gather strength, wished that Sally were there to share it all, and wondered at the strange new vistas opening up inside him.

He had long since learned to live with the responsibility of leadership. Before, he had always known that the answers had come from *him*—from his experience, his intelligence, his ability to see a situation and know the correct answer.

Now was different. Now the answers were not his own. They were from beyond. He *knew* this, knew he was being used as a conduit. It was not a comforting knowledge.

Jake found himself forced to accept his own weaknesses and lack of wisdom. And alongside this were the questions of who was using him, and how he could be sure he was hearing correctly.

The answer was there waiting for him, carried upon a wind which gathered force as the evening's chill took hold. Just as he stood strong and stable upon two legs, so his spiritual foundation needed to be based upon the dual pillars of prayer and daily study of the Scriptures.

In a sudden sweep of understanding, Jake saw beyond his own dilemma to the *opportunity*. By accepting the challenge, he was also being invited to grow. By seeing to the needs of others as well as to his own needs he was given great opportunities to deepen, to have more in order to give more.

A confirming grace of silence descended upon him, as powerful and far-reaching as the star-flecked heavens. Jake climbed back down from the ramparts, carrying the silence with him. This he understood as well. There would often be a need to rest in stillness, to listen without responding, to *wait*. To be sure that the answer was not his own. To give the questions over in prayer and study of the holy pages. To have the strength to remain quiet until the answer was given.

He returned to the stables and found Pierre seated

beside a battered gas cooker, his eyes dark and down-cast. Pierre raised his cup. "They brought the makings for tea. Apparently it is our only heat. Would you like a cup?"

"Sure." Jake squatted down beside the stove. "Beautiful night."

Pierre poured the steaming brew into a mug, added sugar from a small leather sack, and handed it over without meeting Jake's eyes. "You have been a good friend."

"I haven't done anything."

"You have done more than others with a world of words." Pierre raised his gaze. "You have given me the space to think."

Jake sipped the steamy liquid. "Want to tell me about it?"

Pierre's gaze dropped back to the flickering flame. "I feel . . . hollow."

The silence was captivating. Jake found himself hearing it almost as clearly as the words of his friend.

Pierre drew the blanket closer about his shoulders. "There have been moments. I am not sure if I can describe them."

"Try," Jake urged quietly.

"I have spent much time talking to what I am not sure is even there. That is how desperate I have become." Pierre hesitated, and lowered his head farther until his features were lost to shadows. "I am ashamed to tell you."

"No need," Jake said, his voice soft, trying hard to be there without disturbing the peace, the strength of silence.

"There have been moments when the unspoken words of my mind and heart have become alive." Pierre stopped, as though expecting Jake to laugh. When there was no sound, he went on. "I have felt almost as though there was something unseen there, not just listening, but guiding me as well."

Jake took another sip, his eyes steady upon his friend.

"Moments have passed when I am lost to all but the feeling of not being alone. Then the moment goes, and I am left with a greater torrent of doubts and worries than ever before."

Pierre heaved a sigh. "More and more the only peace I can find is in searching my heart's empty spaces with these unspoken words, begging for what I cannot even name to return with this gift of peace. Yet I do not hear the answer I seek. I do not hear what I should do about Jasmyn. Still, this moment of peace is the only answer that makes sense to my fevered mind."

Jake unbuttoned his shirt pocket and drew out his New Testament. "Here."

Pierre raised his head, hesitated, then accepted the book.

"We'll have to share it," Jake said. "It's the only one I have."

"You think I should read this?"

"It's time," he replied. "Begin with Matthew, the first book. If you like, we can talk about what you read."

Pierre fumbled, opened the cover, lowered the volume until its pages were illuminated by the flame. Jake watched him for a moment, his heart filled to bursting. He reached over, set his hand on his friend's shoulder, and offered up a brief prayer of his own. Then he stood and walked to the neighboring stall.

•　　•　　•

Jake awoke to the sound of a cannon's thundering boom. As he swung his feet down from the rich leather seat, a muezzin's cry rose in the chill dawn air. He flung on his clothes, washed in the outdoor trough, checked and saw that Pierre was still asleep, and decided to take his breakfast in the city's market.

He walked through gradually awakening streets, savoring the sights and sounds and smells. Old men greeted the new day seated along sun-dappled walls, hoarding the meager warmth of old bones by wrapping themselves in goat's-hair blankets and sipping loudly from steaming vases of tea.

Jake stood at a tea stall, eating cold unleavened bread and sweet honeyed dates spiced by the flavor of a new world. He was so wrapped up in the moment that when the voice spoke he very nearly cleared both feet from the ground.

"Jake," the voice behind him said.

He spun so fast he spilled the hot liquid over his fingers, shouted his pain, and dropped the vaselike glass. The stall holder cried his outrage when the glass shattered. Immediately Jasmyn spoke soothing words and reached in her belt-purse for coppers. The man subsided under her voice and her beauty, relenting so far as to offer Jake yet another glass.

Gingerly he accepted the tea and demanded of her, "How did you get here?"

"My mother's tribe is from east of these hills," she replied, her proud stature and her quietly spoken English garnering stares from all who passed. "When I was twelve we returned, my mother and I. She was not able to have other children, and she wanted her heritage to live in me. I spent half a year traveling the dry reaches, as long as my mother would remain apart from my father, who was too wedded to the sea ever to travel inland. So it was not hard for me to arrange transport with a hill tribe related to my own."

Jasmyn wore sweeping robes of black, lined with royal blue and a long head scarf of the same rich azure. She accepted her own cup of tea, sipped cautiously, and asked, "How is he?"

"Better," Jake said. "I really think he is better."

Great jade eyes opened to reveal depths of such painful yearning that they twisted his heart. Her voice trembled as much as the hand that held her tea. "Do you think there is a chance for us?"

"I hope so," he said with a fervor that surprised even himself. "But I don't know."

Jasmyn was silent for a time, and when she spoke again her control had returned. "You are in danger, but how much I cannot say."

"How do you know?"

"The Marrakesh jeweler, Herr Reich, was approached by the minions of Ibn Rashid after your departure. Herr Reich found them very willing to accept that he had made a mistake, and that the man with whom he had spoken was not Patrique. Too willing. So he made inquiries. Herr Reich is a well-connected man. It did not take him long to hear that Ibn Rashid had already received word that Patrique was being held for ransom by Sultan Musad al Rasuli."

Jake almost spilled his tea a second time. "He's here?"

"Somewhere," Jasmyn replied quietly, her eyes discreetly focused on the ground at her feet. "I have a relative in the sultan's service. I have sent word that I must speak with him."

"I don't understand," Jake muttered. "The sultan's

assistant was the one who saw us into the city."

"He saw Pierre?"

"He was as close to him as I am to you." Worriedly Jake shook his head. "He's bound to know who's in the prison."

"This I do not understand. But still I believe the information to be true. According to Herr Reich's sources, Ibn Rashid has been arguing for over a month about the bounty demanded by the sultan. He would not do this unless he had solid evidence that Patrique was here. And alive."

She thought a moment. "Pierre must stay hidden as much as he possibly can. There is too much risk of him being recognized."

"That shouldn't be difficult. The official already thinks he's sick."

Concern swept over her features. "Pierre is ill?"

"Only for you," Jake said quietly. "He feels torn in two."

"But you said he was better."

"I hope he is."

"Tell him," she hesitated, and her eyes opened once more to reveal those endless green depths. "Tell him that my heart is his. My heart, my love, my reason for living."

Jake nodded. "How will I find you?"

"Come here again at midafternoon." Slender fingers rose to adjust the folds of her scarf. She then turned and vanished into the swirling throngs.

Jake stood for a long moment, sipping lukewarm tea and marveling at the strength contained in that fragile-seeming woman.

•   •   •

"She said that?"

"Those exact words," Jake confirmed. "She loves you with all her heart. All you have to do is look into her face to see that's the truth."

"And Patrique may be here. So much to think on." Pierre dropped his head into his hands. "I wish I knew—"

"Ah, gentlemens, excellent." Hareesh Yohari appeared in the stable doorway. He stared disdainfully down at Pierre. "Assistant is still with illness?"

"The altitude," Jake said, drawing himself erect. "But he's still working hard, sir."

The little official sniffed. "You come to sultan alone. Better for assistant to stay and work. Now. You have answers to question?"

"Hope so, sir."

"Yes, hope, for you and assistant, I so hope." He motioned. "You come."

Great bronze doors five times the height of a man opened into the inner residence. Geometric mosaics tiled the walls and floors. The air was rich with the fragrance of scented water spouting from a dozen fountains. Hundreds of birds sang from gilded cages. Flowers and palms grew in rich abundance. Servants scuttled in silence along the arched colonnades.

Another set of doors, these of intricately carved sandalwood, were pushed open by a pair of dark-skinned southerners. The official straightened to his full diminutive height and motioned Jake to walk behind him. They passed through stout pillars supporting a domed portico decorated with ivory mosaics. Sharp-eyed courtiers gathered about fountains of sparkling silver grew silent and furtive at his passage. Stern warriors stood at attention, gleaming scimitars at the ready. Peacocks squawked a raucous greeting from tall cages.

A third pair of doors opened before them, these inlaid with intricate patterns of silver and ivory and semiprecious stones. Jake stepped inside, looked up, and gasped. The high dome was layered in sheets of gold.

The official murmured a salutation and bowed low. Jake decided a salute suited him better. When the sultan motioned them forward, Jake proceeded at a stiff-armed march. He approached across a sea of bright carpets, stopped before the dais, and saluted a second time.

The sultan wore an elaborately embroidered cloak of gold and black, sealed at the neck with a ruby the size of a hen's egg. His trousers and curled cloth slippers were sewn with shimmering gold thread. His be-ringed fingers grasped a staff of gold topped with an emerald half the size of Jake's fist. But nothing could disguise the flabby folds of the man's indolent body, nor the cruel glint of his hooded dark eyes.

The staff dipped in Jake's direction and the sultan spoke languidly. His official translated, "Great sultan asks, why you not bow like other mens."

"In my country," Jake replied, still at rigid attention, "the greatest sign of respect a soldier can give to a superior officer is the salute."

"Superior, yes, is good answer." The official turned and replied with a torrent of words and florid hand gestures. As the sultan listened, he gave a tiny flickering motion with one finger. Instantly a servant appeared at his side, stoked the bowl of a silver hookah, set a smoldering coal on the top, then with an elaborate bow handed the sultan the pipe. The sultan sprawled upon his dais, settled within gold-embroidered velvet cushions, and drew hard until the pipe gurgled and threw up great clouds of pungent smoke. Finally satisfied that it was drawing well, he spoke again.

"Great sultan ask, when are cars ready."

"The first should be up and running in two days," Jake replied. "Three at the most."

The official risked a warning glance. "Is best not to be wrong."

"My assistant and I are working around the clock," Jake replied solemnly. "Can't have the great sultan kept waiting."

"No, yes, is true." Hesitantly the official turned back and replied.

The sultan, his face wreathed in smoke, watched Jake. Again Musad al Rasuli spoke. Hareesh translated, "And the other Rolls Royce motor vehicles?"

"A couple of weeks. Probably not more than that."

"Great sultan say, he wait a year, more, and you fix Rolls Royce motor vehicles in days, maybe he keep you here, give you job in stable. Permanent retainer."

"Tell the great sultan it would be an honor to serve him," Jake replied solemnly, keeping his thoughts to himself about being made a slave. Years of dealing with superior officers had taught him that a direct refusal was the worst possible reply to an order.

"Great sultan say, what you expect for these workings."

"The great sultan strikes me as a fair and generous man," Jake replied straight-faced. "Why don't we let him decide what the work is worth."

The official tossed him another uncertain glance, then replied. The sultan contemplatively drew upon his hookah, then motioned his dismissal. Jake threw another exaggerated salute, spun about, and marched back alongside the little official. Only when the great doors had closed behind them did he permit himself a quiet little smile.

Every sense was on full alert as together they went to the rendezvous with Jasmyn that afternoon. His mind shouted danger, but Jake could not refuse Pierre's insistence that he come along. Despite the heat, Pierre wore the black knit cap many older Arabs used against the night chill. With his shoulders hunched, walking half a pace behind and beside Jake, he remained as much hidden as possible.

Jasmyn's calm demeanor dissolved when she spotted Pierre. She rushed up and shepherded them into a refuse-littered alcove between the stalls. "Why do you come?"

"To see you," Pierre replied.

"Oh, oh, oh," she said, reaching for him, pulling back, her face a tormented mask of fear and hope. "How I have dreamed of hearing those words."

"I have thought and I have thought and I have thought," Pierre said, speaking to the stones at his feet. "I speak now so that my friend can hear this as well. Without him I would be lost in the darkness still. I do not know what the answer is, but I know that my life without you is no life at all."

Tears streamed unheeded down her face as she reached with trembling fingers and took one of Pierre's hands in both of hers. Jake blocked them from the view of passersby as much as he could and felt his own heart sing. Jasmyn stroked Pierre's hand and whispered, "Pierre, oh, Pierre."

"Perhaps," Pierre said, his voice unsteady, "perhaps

you can help me to find the answers."

"There is nothing I would rather do," she whispered. "For now, for tomorrow, for all the tomorrows to come."

Jake felt eyes searching his back, probing the shadows where a fair-skinned stranger held the hands of a weeping woman dressed in the garb of the desert tribes. "I think we'd all have a better chance of seeing another tomorrow if we continued this somewhere else."

Pierre nodded. "You will come with us?"

"I cannot," she said, and released one hand long enough to wipe her face. "I would never be permitted entry into the palace grounds. And I have news."

Pierre stiffened. "Patrique?"

She nodded. "He is here."

"But how did the official not recognize me?"

The tears started anew. "I have word that he is not as he once was."

The glint in his eyes turned fierce. "What have they done to him?"

"Pierre," she whispered. "You are hurting me."

Immediately he slackened his clenched fist. "Tell me."

"He is held in the palace dungeon. I have a map." She reluctantly released his hand to extract a slip of paper from the folds of her robe. "There is a barred window high up in his cell wall. It opens onto the yard just beyond the stable courtyard."

"We will find it," Jake said, an idea taking form in his mind.

"You must hurry," she said. "Ibn Rashid's men are said to be here now, striking the final bargain."

"Tonight," Pierre hissed. "My brother will greet the next dawn as a free man."

"But how can you escape?" Her tone became increasingly frantic. "They would shoot you on sight. I could not bear—"

Jake interrupted her with, "Would your people offer us shelter?"

She showed confusion. "How—"

He leaned down. "Would they?"

Jasmyn forced her mind to work. "Some of my mother's tribe are camped at the valley's far eastern end. This I heard from the kinsman who works in the sultan's palace. If I left now, I could be there before nightfall. If I ask for help, they are bound by custom to grant it."

"Better and better," Jake said. "We should be at the road's far eastern end just after dawn tomorrow."

"How is that possible?" She turned to Pierre and begged, "Do not get yourself hurt. If you were to die, I would as well."

He reached for both her hands, held them a moment, then asked Jake, "You have a plan?"

"The bare bones is all."

"Go to your people," Pierre told her. "Tell them we come. Ask them for shelter."

She looked long into his face, drinking in what had so long been denied her. Then she leaned forward and kissed him once, twice, a third time, before releasing him and pulling up her scarf. "Promise me you will come."

"With the dawn," Pierre said, his eyes kindled with a new light. "Now go."

Chapter Sixteen

"They fire a cannon to open and close the main gates?"

Jake stared at his friend. "You really have been out of it, haven't you."

"I don't understand. How can we be sure exactly when it fires?"

"We can't. But the mountains throw the sound back and forth for a while."

"How long?"

"Long enough. That is, if we're ready."

Pierre was silent.

"What do you think?"

He rose to his feet. "I think I need to hear this cannon for myself."

As they walked the crowded ways, Jake told him, "That was a great thing you did, speaking to Jasmyn like that."

"I confess to you and you alone that it would have been impossible without your help, my friend."

"Without God's help, you mean."

"Perhaps," Pierre said, climbing the rampart's ladder behind Jake. "Still, I find it easier to credit you than the Invisible."

They stood in silence and watched the evening descend. When the cannon boomed on cue, Jake counted off the rumbling thunder. "I give it ten, maybe twelve seconds. More than enough time."

"For what?" Pierre demanded.

As night draped the highlands in a blanket of darkness and the immense doors rumbled shut beneath them, Jake outlined his idea. He finished just as the muezzin's wail began to fade. Pierre remained silent for a time, mulling it over in his mind before declaring, "It is a good plan."

"You think it'll work?"

"We can only hope." He clapped his friend on the shoulder and turned for the ladder. "Come. It is time to see if the directions are correct and my brother truly languishes in an Arab's dungeon."

Night cloaked their movements as they walked past the stables and entered a narrow connecting passageway. Eighty meters farther on, the passage opened into a second yard, this one for farm animals. Cows, chickens, ducks, geese, goats, and even a few sheep filled the muddy area with their noise and their smell.

Together the two scouted the surrounding walls and saw, to their immense relief, that the map was correct—no windows faced them from the upper palace walls. They stood and listened to the cacophony and searched the walls of the inner keep.

Jake's guess appeared to be correct—guards were concentrated along the outer keep and within the palace itself. The inner wall was unguarded except for the sentinels at the gate.

They could see only one opening into the palace foundations, a low window just beyond the trough. The air rising through the thick iron bars was so foul that

Jake had trouble approaching. Pierre fell to his knees, clenched the bars, and hissed into the fetid darkness, "Patrique!"

From the pit came a stirring, clinking shuffle. At the sound of chains dragging across stone, the cords of Pierre's neck and arms stretched taut, as though he sought to tear the bars from the wall. He hissed a second time, "Patrique!"

"C'est qui?" came the fearful reply.

"Pierre."

A long pause, then the tremulous murmur, "Mon frère?"

Jake examined the crossbars and knew a qualm of doubt. They were not bolted to the wall, but imbedded deep into the stone. "Ask him if he's chained to the wall."

Pierre did so. The reply wafted upward with the stench. "Oui."

"Three ropes," Jake muttered.

"What?"

"Give him the scoop," Jake replied. "Hurry."

Pierre spoke at length while Jake nervously watched the shadows. Seconds stretched like hours until Pierre sighed, released his hold, and stood. "We go."

When dinner was brought, they sent the servant to summon Hareesh Yohari. The official bustled in more than an hour later, clearly miffed at being disturbed. "What this is, hey? You tell servant go bringing sultan's personal administrator, better having good reason."

Jake straightened, wiping his hands on an oily rag. Pierre kept his burning rage hidden beneath the engine cowling. "This one's almost ready," Jake replied, unable to drag up the pretense of respect. The sound of Patrique's fearful voice rising from the foul darkness hovered still in his mind.

"Yes?" The official was too pleased to note Jake's casual manner. "Is two days early for Rolls Royce motor vehicle to running."

Jake nodded. "We need to take it out for a trial spin tomorrow morning."

Hareesh's brow furrowed. "What this is, trial spin?"

"We need to take the car, the motor vehicle, out to make sure it's running right. You wouldn't want it to break down with the sultan driving, would you?"

The diminutive official showed real horror. "By the Prophet's sword, no, no, is great danger. Heads watching sunset from spike on wall."

"Right. So before the city wakes up and the streets become crowded, just after the cannon fires and the doors open, we'll drive the car out a ways and check it all out. Then we'll bring it back, give it a good polish, and send for you."

Hareesh bobbed his head like a feeding waterbird. "Yes, yes, is smart thinkings. You going for trial before sultan waking."

"Gotcha. You better tell the guards so they don't wonder what we're doing."

"Yes, am telling all peoples tonight."

Jake played it casual, asked the inevitable, "You want to come along?"

Hareesh pretended to give it serious consideration before replying, "No, is not necessary. I drive with sultan." He smiled in utter superiority. "Where are mens to going with car? Valley closed, no roads out, yes?"

"Exactly," Jake agreed, and heaved a great internal sigh as the little official spun on his heel and paraded off.

Pierre chose that moment to extract his grease-smeared face and demand, "Why did you have to ask him that?"

"The only way I could be sure he wouldn't pop up unexpectedly," Jake replied. "The car ready?"

"This car has been perfectly ready," Pierre replied, "for fifteen years."

"Then let's fire the sucker up."

With a new battery and tires and oil and filters, not to mention a careful adjustment by two semiskilled mechanics, the Rolls fired on the first try. Jake swung the cowling closed, fastened the great leather straps, and stepped back. From a dozen paces the sound was barely audible.

He walked over to where Pierre sat behind the wheel. "Who drives tomorrow?"

"You," he replied immediately. "I will be far too nervous."

When their preparations were completed, neither man showed any interest in sleep. They hunkered down by the cooking stove, sipped cups of steaming tea, and silently mused upon what lay ahead.

Finally Pierre raised dark eyes over the rim of his cup and asked, "Do you think it would be a good thing for us to pray?"

"I think it would be a very good thing," Jake said, setting down his cup, realizing he had been half-hoping Pierre would ask. "A very good thing indeed."

Chapter Seventeen

While it was still pitch black, they drove the Rolls through the narrow passage separating their stable from the animal yard. The engine purred with silent grace as Jake eased it forward with scarcely an inch to spare on either side. The yard was quiet save for the bleating of an amiable goat and a single rooster anticipating the dawn. Jake backed the big car up close to the dungeon window, then went back to help Pierre with the ropes.

While his friend lowered the pair of ropes down into the stinking darkness, Jake ran the thickest strand they had found in the stable yards back and forth among the crossed iron bars, then tied both ends to either side of the Rolls' bumper. After carefully testing the knots, he helped Pierre measure out and prepare his own lines. "You better hope your brother understood to tie the longer one to his waist and the shorter one to the wall. Otherwise we're going to stretch him to the limit."

"He understood," Pierre said, frantically tugging on the lines.

"You're sure there's enough play in those lines so they go taut in turn?" Jake cautioned. "The bars have to give first, then the chain is pulled from the wall, then he's raised up to safety. Otherwise—"

"Enough, enough," Pierre hissed, pointing to the lightening sky. "Get into position, Jake. It is almost time."

His heart in his throat, Jake climbed into the quietly idling automobile and waited. Minutes stretched out endlessly, granting him ample time to worry through all the possible things that might go wrong. The sky continued to brighten until he finally decided that the cannon had misfired, that the gates were long since open, that they couldn't hear the muezzin's cry from this end of the palace, that soon a guard was going to appear and point a great blunderbuss down on their heads and—

The cannon's boom caught him totally by surprise. Jake's hand slipped off the gear lever in a sweaty jerk. He fumbled, meshed into first, eased the clutch, and started forward. As the rope connected to the bars pulled taut, he turned back, saw Pierre check the other two and give him a pumping action with one fist. He gunned the engine and willed the bars to give.

Nothing.

The motor roared, the tires spun, Pierre was pelted by a storm of dust and gravel and barnyard filth. His anger mounting, Jake eased off, reversed back, slapped it back into first gear, and tried again. The bars refused to give.

Jake felt something snap in his head. Casting caution to the wind, he slammed the car into reverse, swiveled in his seat, stomped on the accelerator, and roared with the bellowing engine.

He struck the wall with a crashing thud.

Pierre inspected the wall, shouted, "Again!"

A second time he drove forward, raced back, and slammed into the palace.

"Again!"

Jake shouted his frustration and did as he was told.

"Good! Now *pull!*"

Jake rammed the car forward, and the entire section of the wall came away with him.

A second smaller tug signaled that the chain was free from the wall. Jake slowed, turned in the seat, and drove forward while watching back as Pierre fell to his knees by the gaping hole and began guiding the third rope up and out. A shout and Jake stopped and flung open his door. He skidded to a stop at the sight of a herdsman staring wide-eyed at them from the doorway of his stable-yard hovel. Jake opened his jacket to reveal the pistol stuck into his belt, then motioned with his head. The man understood perfectly and vanished back into his hut.

Jake raced back and found Pierre struggling to help a scarecrow of a man clamber up and over the ledge. He was little more than skin and bones and matted beard, clothed in stinking rags. Pierre was almost weeping with rage. "Look at what they have done to my brother."

"He's alive," Jake said tersely. "You want to keep it that way, get him in the car."

Together they bundled Patrique into the back compartment and hid him on the floorboards under a heap of blankets. Jake used his knife to slice the ropes free from the bumper, then returned to where Pierre was tucking blankets around his brother and demanded, "Do you speak English?"

The man was trembling too hard to reply with more than a nod.

"There's a sack of food and water there by your head," Jake went on. "Hold off until we're outside the gates."

Pierre hissed as he shifted the chain still bound to Patrique's leg and revealed great weeping sores circling the ankle.

Jake had opened his mouth to urge Pierre into the front seat when a cry rose from deep in the palace's bowels. They jerked up as further shouts rose from the dungeon, then slammed the passenger door and scrambled into the car. Stiff with alarm, Jake found first gear and slammed the accelerator home.

The Rolls scattered a vast assortment of squawking birds and raced into the narrow passage. Sparks flew from each side in turn as they ricocheted from one stone wall to the other. They exited the passage, roared through the first stable yard, slid into second gear, and passed through the portals of the inner keep at almost thirty miles an hour.

An invading army could scarcely have caused more alarm than the Rolls. Early morning traders, owlish with sleep, cleared their stalls in single bounding leaps at the sight of the great silver eyes roaring down on them. The central passage descended in a series of long sloping steps. Jake managed to clear all four tires a dozen times or more before the great outer doors careened into view. The guards had clearly been forewarned about their intended test drive, for as the car hurtled over the final square and through the portico, they lifted weapons high and shouted their approval. Jake slammed the car into third, took the curve by the river in a dusty four-wheel spin, and roared away.

The road leading east was rough and cobblestoned and blindingly bright from the sun's rising glare. Jake was literally on top of the first goat before he saw the herd, and carried two of the animals a good thirty yards before he managed to shake them loose. He then remembered that the car probably had a horn, and hit every surface on the dash before discovering the switch by his right hand. He then drove by horn and feel, his eyes squinted up against the blazing orb. The horn was a splendid three-tone affair, blaring out its royal aaah-oooh-gah in time to their jouncing progress.

To Jake's relief, the road took a gentle turning, and a high central peak blocked the sun. Jake managed a swift glance at his companion. Pierre sat wide-eyed and rigid as the car frame. Jake shouted, "You all right?"

"How fast are we going?"

Jake checked the controls, replied, "A little over seventy."

"You will never speak to me about my driving again," Pierre shouted back. "Is that clear?"

Jake grinned and swerved to avoid a shepherd glued to the center of the road with terror. His sheep had shown more sense and were scattered to the wind. The mountains were drawing closer, shielding them from the dawn's glare. They passed through two villages in turn, the villagers frozen to the ground. Jake had sufficiently recovered by then to bestow a few regal waves as they breezed bumpily through.

They were almost upon the mountains before Pierre pointed and shouted, "The cliff at eleven o'clock!"

Jake craned and spotted the blue-robed Arab waving and pointing them toward a crevice opening at his feet. Without slowing, Jake wheeled the big car off the rapidly deteriorating road. The engine roared in mighty fury as the tires spun through softer sand before catching hold and hurtling forward. Careening wildly from side to side, Jake scrambled through the yielding drift, willing the car onward. The steep rock side rose up around them, and they hit harder ground. Jake eased up on the accelerator as they hurtled ever deeper into the rock-walled crevass.

They continued on this winding course for almost ten miles before the walls closed in so tightly they threatened to jam the car to a halt. Another sharp turning, and suddenly the walls opened to reveal a great open space where tall date palms sheltered an open well. At the car's unexpected appearance, camels reared, sheep scattered, goats bleated, and Arabs came streaming toward them.

Jake was too caught up in the adrenaline rush to just sit there. He slammed back the roof, stepped up on the seat, raised two fists high over his head, and shouted up at the heavens above, *"Yee-ha!"*

"My cousin says your greeting is worthy of a great warrior," Jasmyn said, hastening forward, her eyes fastened upon Pierre. At her side strode a tall Arab of proud bearing and evident strength. "My cousin, Omar Al-Masoud, leader of the Al-Masoud tribe, bids you welcome."

Jake grinned down at the pair. "Tell your cousin we're mighty grateful for his hospitality, and ask him if he's in the market for a slightly used Rolls Royce. We'd like him to accept it as a little token of appreciation and all that."

Dark eyes gleamed brightly at the translation. He stared up at Jake for a long moment, then nodded once. Jake felt a thrill of having gotten something very important very right. "My cousin asks if this is the sultan's car."

"It was."

"Then he accepts your gift and asks if you can drive it into the cave there behind you."

"No problem." Jake watched Pierre step from the car and walk stiffly over to Jasmyn. She stared up at him, searching his face for a long time. The Arab observed the scene with an unreadable gaze. Pierre nodded once, then said quietly, "At times I wondered if perhaps my memories had painted you to be more beautiful than you were. No one could be so lovely, I told myself. But I see that I was wrong to wonder."

Jasmyn lifted one hand to touch his face, then stopped herself. Her voice was shaky as she said, "I have told my people that you are my fiance. It does the tribe honor to have me return with you before, before . . ."

"Before our marriage," Pierre said quietly.

She gasped a single quick sob, but with great determination drew herself up. "They will help us go where we wish."

"A doctor," Jake said, motioning to the back compartment. "Patrique is in pretty bad shape."

Jasmyn turned and spoke to her cousin, who called over a pair of women. Pierre tore himself away from Jasmyn to help them bring Patrique out. "There is a healer two villages away," Jasmyn translated. "We will go there."

"Jasmyn," Patrique murmured. "Is it truly you?"

She walked over and touched the gaunt man's trembling hand. "You are safe now, my friend."

"Again you have saved me," he said hoarsely. "How can I ever repay you?"

Pierre started. "Again?"

"There is no debt, and thus nothing to repay," Jasmyn replied.

"Because of her I escaped from Marseille just ahead of the Nazi raid," Patrique said. "How can you not know of this?"

"Because I am a fool," Pierre replied, gazing at her.

A call hallooed from above and beyond the rocky confines. A guard above their heads called back and away from them. A distant call drifted back upon the wind. The entire camp seemed to hold its breath and listen. "Horses," Jasmyn said. "Many horses. Coming this way."

Omar shouted instructions. Jake saw a group gather up branches and began brushing away the car's tracks. "Please, Jake," Jasmyn urged, "you are to drive the car into the cave now. We must hurry. The sultan's men are after us."

Chapter Eighteen

I t was three days before Omar felt safe enough to bring them into a village. They walked twenty miles or more each day, passing through narrow defiles which opened suddenly into boulder-strewn pastures. Always their destination at day's end was pasture and water. Seldom was there warning before the rocky gorges spilled them into the great open spaces. Their path wound through chasms and passes and bone-dry valleys, jinking back and forth so repeatedly that Jake could never have found his way out alone. Somewhere up ahead, Omar told him through Jasmyn, the jagged Atlas foothills joined the Sahara. There in the first desert reaches waited the remainder of his tribe. That was their destination. For now, they took a course uncharted by any save those trained by their fathers, and they by their fathers before them. Such, proclaimed Omar, was the desert way.

They met other people only once in that three-day stretch, another desert tribe sending wool and hand-woven carpets toward Telouet. Jake crouched in the shadows of the great central tent, dressed in the same desert robes as all the other men, and watched as solemn greetings were exchanged.

Patrique rode hunched on a camel, recovering slowly, sleeping much and eating with the hunger of one who could never be sated. Pierre and Jasmyn tended to him constantly, but in truth Jake felt they saw little save each other. He did not mind. A whole new world opened up before him, one of silence and heat and sun and wind. Omar saw that Jake's fascination was genuine and accepted him into the fold. Their lack of a common tongue was no great barrier. Speech was not so important here in the reaches where silence reigned.

On the third day, Omar entered the quiet stucco village with Jake and Jasmyn. Pierre had elected to remain behind with Patrique. Jake wore the royal blue of the desert tribes, belted and robed and turbaned. The clothes still carried a hint of alienness with them, but they no longer hung as strangely as they had the first day. Jake was swiftly learning to appreciate them and the life they stood for.

The village was composed of two dozen meager huts, more camels than people, and more goats than both. A single wire strung limply from pole to pole connected the village with the outside world.

They followed the wire to the village's main store, a fly-infested pair of rooms stocking everything from saddles to salt. Barefoot children in filthy miniature robes scampered in the dust outside the doorway. Jake walked in after Omar, waited while the formal greetings were exchanged, and watched the storekeeper enter into a paroxysm of refusal when Omar made his request. Not content to simply shake his head, the storekeeper rose to his feet and twisted his entire body back and forth. Although Jake could not understand a word, the message was clear. Under no circumstances would he allow a stranger to send a telegraph on his set. No matter that the storekeeper could only send and receive in Arabic. The message must be translated and sent by him, the one and only official telegraph operator in the valley.

Jake then reached into his belt pouch and displayed his dwindling wad of dollars. The storekeeper deflated like a punctured balloon. His entire demeanor changed. He pushed open the stall door, shoved papers and forms and sheets off the cluttered desk and onto the floor, dusted off his chair, and held it as Jake sat down.

Through Jasmyn Jake made his request. No, the storekeeper replied, there was no problem in making a connection to Gibraltar. Of course, he had never done it, but yes, it was possible through the operator in Tangiers. They had communicated several times, and he knew the operator to be a good man. Yes, of course, for the desert sahib he could make the connection. It would be an honor. One moment, please.

They waited out the interim in the shadowed coolness of the village's only teahouse, which in truth was simply the front room of the shopkeeper's own three-room shanty. As they sat and sipped the sugary tea, Jasmyn said, "We have been ignoring you these past few days."

"You have every reason to," Jake replied. "I'm not much competition for true love."

Dark green eyes raised to gaze at him. "I am in your debt," she said gravely. "You have restored to me my reason for living."

"Not me," Jake countered. "It was all God's work."

"Yes, I have heard the same from Pierre," she said, "and this is as great a miracle as the fact that he is here with me." She watched Jake for a long moment, then asked, "Could you perhaps teach me how to find God so that I may thank Him?"

"There is nothing on earth," Jake replied sincerely, "that would give me greater joy."

The moment became almost an hour before the storekeeper, now swelled with importance, announced that his Tangiers connection, whose name by the way was Mohammed, had succeeded in making the link to the central Gibraltar operator, who happened to be at the naval base. Oh, that was exactly the person with whom the sahib wished to speak? Then indeed Allah must be smiling on their proceedings. Please, please, the sahib must now sit and communicate with the Gibraltar operator.

Jake approached the telegraph key with trepidation. He had no hope of arriving back on time, and his commanding officer was a firebrand for discipline. Jake knew there was a very good chance that General Clark would tear his story apart, especially with him not there to defend it. But he had too much respect for the general to offer anything but the truth. He hoped fervently that Bingham would weigh in on his behalf and confirm at least the beginning of their journey.

He unfolded the paper bearing the message he had composed the night before, bent over the key, and began. It took almost forty-five minutes to transcribe the message, partly because it was long and partly because his Morse code was so rusty. When he finished, Jake sighed his way to his feet, unbent his back, and said, "I guess we might as well go."

The storekeeper accepted the dollars with unbridled greed. He salaamed repeatedly and shook each of their hands half a dozen times before finally permitting them to depart.

They were almost at the outskirts of the village before the cry rose up behind them. "Sahib, sahib!"

The storekeeper raced up, fought for breath, and jabbered away while plucking at Jake's sleeve. "He has received a reply from Gibraltar," Jasmyn told Jake. "He cannot understand it, and says you must come back now."

Jake raced back to the store, slid into the seat, and keyed in the repeat sign. The reply came back immediately:

BINGHAM HERE STOP HAVE BEEN IN FREQUENT TOUCH WITH CLARK STOP NUMEROUS DEVELOPMENTS THIS SIDE STOP REQUEST CONFIRMATION THAT BROTHER OF MAJOR SERVAIS ALIVE AND WELL STOP

Jake pushed aside all wonderment and keyed back:

PATRIQUE ALIVE AND RECOVERING FROM ORDEAL STOP IS HERE WITH US STOP

ASSUME FROM YOUR MESSAGE THAT TRAVEL BACK TO TANGIERS OR RABAT IMPOSSIBLE STOP

AFFIRMATIVE STOP WE ARE HUNTED BOTH BY IBN RASHID AND THE SULTAN'S MEN STOP

A longer pause, then:

URGENT YOU AND MAJOR SERVAIS ESCORT HIS BROTHER TO PORT OF MELILLA STOP WILL HAVE BOAT RENDEZVOUS WITH YOU

THERE STOP EXTREME CAUTION REQUIRED
STOP REQUEST ETA STOP

Jake turned to Jasmyn and asked, "Ask Omar if he
can take us to Melilla."

Her eyes widened, as did his at the translation. "You
seek to cross the Hamada and the Jebel Sahara? Those
reaches are called the Great Burn. They are most dangerous."

"Does he know if it is possible?"

Omar drew himself up to full height. Through Jasmyn he replied, "I hold the desert wisdom of twenty
generations. No one but I could see you across the Hamada hill country and the eastern Sahara. No one."

Jake recognized a negotiating ploy when he heard
one. "Hang on a sec." He keyed out:

HAVE POSSIBLE GUIDE AND COVER BUT EX-
PENSIVE STOP

BOAT WILL CARRY ADEQUATE SUM AND AU-
THORITY FOR PAYMENT STOP REQUEST ETA
STOP

"We will pay you well," Jake replied to Omar. When
that was translated he asked Jasmyn, "Would you come
with us?"

"Pierre will be traveling with you?"

"I think so. And Patrique."

"Then I will go." Definite. Unequivocal. Determined.

"Ask him how long it would take, please."

The translated reply came back, "Two weeks if the
wind and Allah are with us. If not," Omar shrugged his
reply.

UNDER A MONTH STOP

TOO LONG STOP YOU ARE HEREBY COM-
MANDED TO MAKE FOR MELILLA WITH ALL
POSSIBLE HASTE STOP WILL CLEAR WITH
YOUR SUPERIORS THIS SIDE STOP CONFIRM
BROTHER OF MAJOR SERVAIS HAS PROOF OF
TRAITOR STOP

AFFIRMATIVE STOP BUT HE IS ILL AND MAY
SLOW US DOWN STOP

MAKE HASTE BUT WITH PRUDENCE STOP
HOW RECEIVED STOP

LOUD AND CLEAR STOP

GODSPEED